Praise for

SCARLET
and
IVY

"This is one of the best books I have ever read. It was exciting, funny, warm and mysterious." **Lily, aged 9**

"The whole book was brilliant... after the first paragraph it was as though Ivy was my best friend." **Ciara, aged 10**

"This book is full of excitement and adventure – a masterpiece!" **Jennifer, aged 9**

"This is a page-turning mystery adventure with puzzles that keep you guessing." **Felicity, aged 11**

"A brilliant and exciting book." **Evie, aged 8**

"The story shone with excitement, secrets and bonds of friendship... If I had to mark this book out of 10, I would give it 11!" **Sidney, aged 11**

SOPHIE CLEVERLY was born in Bath in 1989. She wrote her first story at the age of four, though it used no punctuation and was essentially one long sentence. Thankfully, things have improved somewhat since then, and she has earned a BA in Creative Writing and MA in Writing for Young People from Bath Spa University.

Now working as a full-time writer, Sophie lives with her partner in Wiltshire, where she has a house full of books and a garden full of crows.

Books by Sophie Cleverly

The Scarlet and Ivy series
in reading order

THE LOST TWIN

THE WHISPERS IN THE WALLS

THE DANCE IN THE DARK

THE LIGHTS UNDER THE LAKE

THE CURSE IN THE CANDLELIGHT

SCARLET
and
IVY

The Lost Twin

SOPHIE CLEVERLY

HarperCollins *Children's Books*

First published in the United Kingdom by HarperCollins *Children's Books* 2015
HarperCollins *Children's Books* is a division of HarperCollins*Publishers* Ltd,
HarperCollins *Publishers*
1 London Bridge Street
London SE1 9GF

HarperCollins*Publishers*
Macken House, 39/40 Mayor Street Upper,
Dublin 1, D01 C9W8 Ireland

This edition published in 2016
54

www.harpercollins.co.uk

Scarlet and Ivy : The Lost Twin
Text copyright © Sophie Cleverly, 2015
Illustration copyright © Manuel Šumberac, 2015

Sophie Cleverly asserts the moral right to be identified as the author of this work.

978-0-00-758918-0

Printed and bound in the UK using
100% Renewable Electricity at CPI Group (UK) Ltd

For Mum and Dad, who made everything possible.
For Ed: we have everything to look forward to.

Chapter One

This is the story of how I became my sister.

I got the letter on September the first. I remember that because it was the day after our thirteenth birthday. *My* thirteenth birthday. The first one I wouldn't share with my twin sister, Scarlet.

I woke up and made my way down the winding stairs of my aunt Phoebe's house, breathing in the smell of bacon cooking as I went. The early morning sun was already warming the air. It could have been a good day.

As I emerged from the shadow of the stairs and into the sunlit hallway, I noticed it. An envelope lying on the stone floor.

For a moment I thought it might be a belated birthday card – the only card I'd had that year was from my aunt, and looking at the single, lonely name written at the top had hurt more than I could say – but as I picked the envelope up it felt more like a letter.

Scarlet had always liked to send me secret messages, but she sealed her letters so haphazardly that you could probably have opened hers just by breathing on them. This one was closed tightly and sealed with wax. I turned it over and saw that it was addressed to my aunt. *I ought to open it*, I thought. Aunt Phoebe didn't object to me reading her post. In fact, it was usually necessary; she just let it pile up in the hallway if I didn't.

I went into the kitchen and sat down on one of the rickety chairs. I took a closer look at the seal on the envelope – it was black, with a raised imprint of a bird on top of an oak tree. The words 'Rookwood School' were stamped underneath in dark-coloured ink.

Rookwood School. Scarlet's school. Why were they writing to Aunt Phoebe?

I slid a butter knife from the drawer along the envelope.

Mrs Phoebe Gregory
Blackbird Cottage
Bramley Hollow

30th August, 1935

Dear Mrs Gregory,

As you are the guardian of Ivy Grey, I am writing to inform you that in light of recent unfortunate circumstances a place has become available at our school, and your niece will take it. Her parents have fully paid the fees and she is due to start as soon as possible. A teacher will be sent to collect her and the details will be explained upon her arrival.

Regards,

Edgar Bartholomew (Headmaster)

I threw the letter down as if it had singed my fingers. Could they really be referring to my sister's death as 'unfortunate circumstances'?

I sat and stared at it, questions racing through my head. For some reason, Rookwood School wanted me – the twin who wasn't good enough. Surely there were hundreds of other girls they could give the place to. Why me?

It was then that I noticed that the smell of bacon cooking had turned into the smell of bacon burning. I jumped up and ran to the iron stove, waving the smoke away from my face. It was too late; the bacon was already cremated.

Aunt Phoebe must have wandered off somewhere in the middle of cooking. This was a common occurrence. I glanced out of the kitchen window and spotted her sitting on the bench in the garden, her hands folded neatly in her lap and a faraway expression on her face. Aunt Phoebe's husband had died in the Great War, leaving behind only a study full of books and a small pension for my aunt. She hadn't been quite the same since.

I grabbed the letter and went outside. My aunt didn't look around even though my footsteps crunching on the gravel betrayed my presence. She was watching the goldfish in the pond. Little ripples curled as they bobbed to the surface and then darted away, their golden scales glinting in the sun.

"Aunt Phoebe?"

"Oh, Ivy," she replied, blinking up at me, and then returning her gaze to the water. "I didn't see you there, dear."

"You got a letter from—" I started, but my aunt interrupted, seemingly unaware that I had spoken.

"Scarlet loved the fish, didn't she? I remember when you were little, she used to kneel by the pond and make faces at her reflection. She always said that it was like another twin, only even wetter than you."

I gave a weak smile. *Typical Scarlet*. She made fun of

everyone, and me the most, but I never thought anything of it. Or tried not to, anyway.

Scarlet and I were mirror twins. Before we were born, our mother thought she was having only one baby, but then I arrived – a slightly smaller and weaker version of my sister, but a perfect mirror image. Our birthmarks were the same but on opposite sides. I was left-handed while Scarlet was right-handed. Aunt Phoebe's husband, Doctor Gregory, had once told me that our hearts might be reversed too. I was like Scarlet's reflection come to life.

I sat beside Aunt Phoebe on the bench. It wasn't surprising that my aunt's thoughts were of Scarlet. She had always been everyone's favourite, bold and brash and outgoing. I was just Ivy. *Shy, clingy Ivy*. I could have been Scarlet's reflection, but I might as well have been her shadow.

"Oh goodness, I am sorry," Aunt Phoebe said. "I was just reminded of her."

"I understand," I said.

But I didn't. I didn't understand why Scarlet had died. I didn't understand how someone so full to the brim with life could be gone. I didn't understand why God, if he was up there, would give me a twin only to take her away again.

Or that somehow the world was still carrying on.

"You got a letter," I repeated, waving it at her.

Aunt Phoebe looked up. "Oh? What does it say?"

"They want me to go to Rookwood. To take Scarlet's place."

Her eyes widened considerably. "Well, gosh." She paused. "That's quite an honour. It's a prestigious school, isn't it?"

Rookwood School. Barely a few months ago, just before the summer had begun, Scarlet had died there. A sudden fever, they said, flu or pneumonia; something that couldn't have been predicted or prevented. My stepmother casually told me these explanations as I sobbed, as if they meant nothing, when half of my world had just been torn away.

I never wanted to go to that place. Not now, *not ever.*

I looked up at my aunt, her gentle face framed by greying hazel curls. "And your father has already agreed to it?"

I sighed. It was just like him to agree such a thing without telling me. "According to the letter. It says the fees have been paid in full."

"Well, then it's decided, my dear," said Aunt Phoebe.

I didn't reply.

"I'll leave you to think about it," she said brightly, patting me on the leg. Then she wandered off down the garden path, past the privy and the vegetable patch, and began pulling weeds. She started to sing quietly to herself, already a world away.

I felt helpless, like I was being slowly dragged towards Rookwood, a place only seen in my imagination, but nonetheless it filled me with terror.

Maybe it will be a good thing, I tried to tell myself. *A new start, new friends*. Any *friends*. After all, Scarlet had always said she wished that I could join her there. I would be closer to her there, somehow, wouldn't I?

Without warning, I started to cry and hastily wiped the tears from my cheeks. Who was I kidding? The last place on earth I wanted to go was the place where Scarlet had... Just thinking about it made my head pound.

I threw the stupid letter on to the grass.

Aunt Phoebe looked up, clutching a handful of straggly dandelions. I put my head in my hands and heard her walking back towards me down the gravel path.

"Oh, Scarlet," she said, looking over me with blank eyes. "I'm sure you'll be all right going to this school. I'll miss you terribly, of course, but you *will* be fine on your own, won't you?"

She didn't even notice her mistake.

I didn't think I would *ever* be fine on my own.

Chapter Two

It was a bright day that followed, one of those where it feels so hot and hazy that you can't believe the summer is coming to an end. I was lying flat on my back on the stone edge of the pond, reading a tattered copy of *Jane Eyre* and trying my best to forget about my impending Rookwood fate.

Sometimes I would look into the water just to see my green-tinged reflection staring back at me. It was almost enough to pretend Scarlet was right there with me.

Almost.

"Ivy!" My aunt's voice rang out from the back door.

I sat up so quickly I almost dropped the book in the pond.

"Ivy!" she called again, despite the fact that I was looking straight at her. She was wringing the ends of her apron in her pale hands.

"Yes?" I answered.

"You've got a... visitor. It's a teacher from the school."

So soon? I wasn't ready for this now. But then, maybe I never would be. I cautiously walked back to the cottage, curling my toes over the hard stones.

"A lady," she added, before gently pushing me into the kitchen.

The *lady* was tall and skinny, and wore a long dress that looked several sizes too large. It was black and covered with pockets. Her face was sharp and pointed, and her brown hair was pulled into a tight bun that made it look like she had a row of clothes pegs on the back of her head, pinching her skin tighter. It was not a particularly pleasant face to look at, especially given that she was fixing me with the expression of someone who has just chewed a rotten wasp.

"Ivy Grey?" she said.

"Yes?" I replied, stunned.

"Yes *Miss*. I trust that you have received our letter?"

"Yes, Miss." I nodded carefully, and watched as she stalked around the kitchen table. She ran a finger along the surface, then scrutinised it in a most unladylike manner. "Good. Then you will accompany me to the school."

I blinked. "Right now?"

The woman lowered her eyebrows and folded her bony arms. "Yes, right now. It is the beginning of the term. Therefore, you are supposed to be at school."

I turned around, and saw my aunt standing there, wide-eyed.

"Aunt Phoebe?" I said, giving her a pleading look.

"Excuse us a moment," she said to the teacher, gently pulling me back into the hallway. "Oh, my dear," she said quietly. "She does seem strict, but it is a very good school, and they're bound to be rather, um..."

"But Aunt Phoebe..." I whispered, "I-I thought there'd be more time." Truth be told, I was a bit worried about my aunt being all alone too. "And what about you?" I asked.

My aunt smiled vacantly. "I'll get along just fine."

I peered back through the door at the horrible sharp woman, who was tapping her foot and glaring at me with squinty eyes.

"I haven't got all day," she said, haughtily. "Go and get your things." She gestured upstairs, the contents of her pockets jangling as she moved.

Scarlet would have stamped on that tapping foot. But me – well, I did as I was told.

I climbed the stairs with a shudder. Everything about that ghastly woman in the kitchen made me nervous.

My bedroom was through a little doorway off the landing, built for someone a great deal smaller than me. It had a low-beamed ceiling and a window with warped panes of glass. When I came to stay at Aunt Phoebe's house, it had seemed so lonely at first; obvious that there was no room for a twin. But it had grown to feel like home, and I was sad to be leaving it.

I reached under the bed to find my blue carpet bag. I filled it with my few possessions – a comb, toiletries, metal hair-curling clips, stationery and ink, some books, the half string of tiny pearls that I had inherited from our mother, Emmeline. She had died shortly after giving birth to Scarlet and I, so we never knew her. Maybe if she had been there to look after us, Scarlet would still be alive now.

I threw in my underclothes and my best dress – all of which bore the strong scent of lavender from Aunt Phoebe's drawer liners – even though I knew that I would be required to wear a uniform at Rookwood School. I took out my ballet clothes, the cream leotard and skirt, and the black set too. I wrapped the soft pink shoes in tissue paper before packing them. They were almost new, and I prayed they would last a few months at least.

It had taken no time at all to pack the contents of my life.

Now the little room looked bare and sad. As I laced up my leather shoes I stared at the floorboards, trying to convince myself everything was going to be all right.

You'll be fine. There's nothing to be afraid of. It's only a school.

I shut my eyes and took a deep, shaky breath. And then I traipsed back downstairs with my bag.

"Are you ready to go?" Aunt Phoebe asked. "I'm sure Mrs... Miss, I'm sorry, what did you say your name was?"

"Miss Fox," snapped the woman.

"I-I'm sure Miss Fox will look after you," Aunt Phoebe said, without raising her gaze to meet my eyes. She placed a hand on my shoulder, reassuringly. "I'll see you soon, Ivy, my dear," she added, planting a kiss on my forehead.

"I hope so," I said, managing a smile. "I'll write."

Miss Fox's foot began tapping even faster. "We haven't got time for niceties. The driver is waiting."

I winced and clutched hold of my bag more tightly, then I followed Miss Fox into the lane, where the bright sunshine hit my eyes.

"Goodbye, darling," said my aunt.

"Goodbye," I mouthed back. And before I knew it, I was being bundled into the back of an expensive-looking motor car.

The smell of leather seats and the smoke from the driver's

cigar hit my nose instantly.

"Sit up," snapped Miss Fox, as she climbed into the front.

"I'm sorry, miss?"

She turned and looked at me as if I were a sick sheep. "Sit up straight when you're in my vehicle. And kindly avoid touching the seats."

I folded my hands in my lap and began to ask, "How long will it take to—"

"Quiet!" she interrupted. "All this senseless chatter is giving me a headache."

The engine chugged into life as I leant back and tried to take some deep breaths, but the fumes made me cough. Miss Fox tutted loudly.

All I could see of the driver was a flat tweed cap and the grey hair on the back of his neck. He said nothing, simply nodded and pulled away.

I peered out of the back window, and saw Aunt Phoebe standing on the doorstep. She gave me a sad wave. I watched her shrink as we drove, fading into the sunlight that streamed through the trees.

I turned around, and saw my eyes reflected in the driver's mirror. They were brimming with tears.

Chapter Three

The car wove its way through the twisting country lanes. Miss Fox sat bolt upright in the front seat, barely blinking as the wheels bumped through ruts in the road. I fidgeted in the back, thinking it strange that she had chosen to sit up front with the driver.

On a few occasions she turned around to give me a look, and I tried to avoid her eye. Eventually she turned her angry gaze on the passing countryside instead, allowing me back into my own world.

The trouble was that my world was filled with Scarlet. Everything we passed in the familiar landscape reminded me of her. The way she used to hop over wooden stiles, while I dangled my legs over warily. The way she used to pick the green leaves off the bushes and crush them into tiny pieces. The way she used to smile at the blue sky, pointing out the shapes in the clouds that only she could see.

The worst was when I noticed two girls, perhaps sisters, playing together in a garden. I felt the memory flow through me, and as hard as I tried, it wouldn't stop coming. The day Scarlet left for school...

We were standing there on the lawn, each with our matching suitcases; Scarlet in her uniform, me in a plain pink dress.

Father wanted to send us away. "Time to get an education," he said. "Time to become proper young ladies," he said. But Scarlet had won a place, and I hadn't. So they were sending her to Rookwood School, and me to stay with Aunt Phoebe. Father waved goodbye to us with a glass of whisky in his hand. Our stepmother, wearing a pinafore and a grimace, dismissed us without even a second glance as she fussed over her sons, our stepbrothers.

Maybe Aunt Phoebe was a better alternative to our parents, but she was strange and scatterbrained. You could never tell what she was thinking.

There on the lawn, with the suitcases, I knew what Scarlet was thinking. She wished that we were both going to the school, so she wouldn't have to go alone. I knew she was thinking that, because I was thinking it too. I started to cry; big, gulping, childish sobs.

Scarlet took my hand. "Don't worry, Ivy-Pie," she said bravely. "I'll write you a letter every week. And you'll write me one back. And when I've finished school I'll come and get you, and we'll run away together and become beautiful actresses, or prima ballerinas, only we'll be even more famous because we're twins. And we can go to America, and everyone in the whole world will want to be our friend."

I cried even harder. Because it was ridiculous, and I would miss the ridiculous things that Scarlet came out with. Not only that, but because we both knew that I would never become famous and loved by everyone.

That destiny could only be Scarlet's.

I wiped away a tear and quietly folded my knees up on the seat, risking further tutting from Miss Fox. But she didn't notice, so I stayed curled up there, trawling through my memories.

Scarlet making a fortress from blankets, protecting her dolls from the Viking Hordes. (That would be me. I wasn't much of a horde.)

Scarlet leaving trails of painted Easter eggs around our garden, making me find them with clues and riddles. (Our stepbrothers always tried to smash them.)

Scarlet brushing her hair for a hundred strokes before she would let me plait it.

Scarlet hunched over her diary, scribbling away, her tongue poking out of the corner of her mouth.

My sister always wrote in her diary. Every little event had to be pinned to the page. I never saw the point of it then, but she always said that if she didn't write down everything that happened, it would just disappear forever. There would be no one to remember.

I told her that I would remember, always, but she just laughed and took no notice.

I started picking at the stitching of the seat nervously. There was no way that Scarlet would have been afraid in this situation. She would have taken it in her stride, asked all the questions I wanted answers to. But Ivy Grey never asked questions. Well, not difficult ones anyway. I always just did as I was told.

"Stop that, child," Miss Fox hissed. "And sit properly!"

I looked up from my lap, but she had already turned away.

Scarlet would have answered back. Scarlet would have drummed her feet on the seats. Scarlet would have ripped out every bit of that stupid stitching.

I did as I was told.

Soon the road widened, and more houses slid into view. I saw a dark-haired man digging his garden, wiping the sweat from his brow with a handkerchief. His beard and strong features reminded me of Father, and I felt a sudden pang of guilt – I hadn't even spoken to him for months. He was working in London, I supposed. The economy was still reeling from the Crash and it had left him working all the hours he could.

It wasn't as if I was close to our father. When we were younger, he had been a fiery man, always shouting. But soon after our stepmother came along, he became different. Scarlet was relieved; she was grateful for the peace, didn't miss the fire. She could never understand why I would prefer the man who shouted at us to the man who spent long hours withdrawn, blank-faced.

With three boys to spoil, our stepmother swiftly decided it was too much for her to keep looking after us as well. That was when she suggested that he ship us off to boarding school.

If only he hadn't sent us away. If only we'd stayed together.

If only...

The car slid through a pair of enormous gates. Beside them were pillars topped with stone rooks in flight, their wings spread wide and claws grasping at the air.

A long drive snaked its way up to the school, through a cloak of trees and past what looked like a lake shimmering in the distance. We came to a halt and I heard the driver's feet hit the gravel as he climbed out.

"Watch your step, miss," he said, pulling open the door.

I smiled up at him as best I could as I clambered out with my bag.

Rookwood School loomed over me, huge and imposing. The bright green trees that lined the drive looked lost in the gloom of the building. The walls were stone – the highest parts blackened by years of chimney smoke. Dark pillars stretched towards the sky in front of me, and crenellations framed the vast slate roof.

It looked like a castle. Or a prison.

It took all my strength not to turn and run back down the length of the drive. Of course, even if I had, I would surely have been caught and punished.

Rooks flew past overhead, their loud caws mixing with the distant shrieks of girls playing hockey.

"Don't just stand there gaping, girl." Miss Fox was

looking at me like I was an unexpected slug on the sole of her shoe. "Follow me, unless you think you have something better to do."

"Yes, Miss... no, Miss."

She turned around, muttering something that I couldn't hear.

I followed her up the front steps, her sharp shoes clacking and pockets jangling. The front doors were huge, and despite being ancient they swung open without even the smallest creak when she pushed through them. Inside there was a double-height room with a gallery running all the way around. It smelt strongly of floor polish.

In the middle sat an oak desk and a somewhat lost-looking secretary. She was shuffling papers in what I thought was an attempt to look busier than she actually was.

Miss Fox approached the desk and leant on it with both hands.

"Good afternoon, madam," the secretary said quietly, as Miss Fox's shadow fell across her.

"Some would say so," replied Miss Fox, glowering. "I have a child here. Scarlet Grey." I started to correct her, but she waved an uncaring hand in my face and carried on speaking. "She will begin attending classes tomorrow. Sign her in on the register, please."

Miss Fox must have been the only person who could

pronounce the word 'please' like it actually meant 'RIGHT NOW'.

"D-do you want me to escort her to her room, madam?" asked the secretary.

Miss Fox blinked. "No, I am going to take her to my office to... fill her in. Get her signed up."

She strode away towards the corridor and I hurried after her. I risked a backward glance at the secretary, who stared at me with wide eyes.

We went past rows of doors, each with a little window revealing the class studying inside. The girls were sat in rows, silent and serious. I was used to a quiet school, but in here there was an air of... *wrongness*. Like it was too quiet, somehow.

The only sounds were our footsteps and the ever-present jangling from Miss Fox's pockets. When we reached her office, she pulled out a silver key from one of them and unlocked the door.

The room was dimly lit and smelt of old books. There was a single desk with a couple of high-backed chairs and some tall shelves. That was pretty normal, but that wasn't all there was.

The walls were covered in *dogs*.

Big dogs, small dogs, strange foreign dogs – their blank sepia faces stared down from faded photographs, each in a brown frame. In one corner of the room there was a stuffed beagle in a glass case, its droopy ears and patchy fur serving to make it look even more depressed than beagles do when they're alive.

The most bizarre sight was a dachshund, stretched out in front of the small window at the back of the office. It appeared to be being used as a draught excluder.

Strange, I thought, *that someone with a name like Fox would like dogs so much.*

"Stuffed dogs, Miss?" I wondered aloud.

"Can't stand the things. I like to see them dead," replied Miss Fox.

She pointed a long finger at a nearby chair until I got the hint and sat down on it.

"Now, Scarlet—"

"Ivy," I corrected automatically.

She loomed over me like an angry black cloud. "I think you have misunderstood, Miss Grey. Did you not read my letter?"

Her letter? "I-I thought it was from the headmaster."

She shook her head. "Mr Bartholomew has taken a leave of absence, and I am in charge while he's away. Now, answer the question. Did you read it?"

"Yes. It said I was to take a place at the school... my sister's place."

Miss Fox walked around me and sat down in the leather chair that accompanied her desk. "Precisely. You will replace her."

Something in the way she said it made me pause. "What do you mean, replace her, Miss?"

"I mean what I say," she said. "You will replace her. You will *become* her."

Chapter Four

I gasped. "No," I whispered. "What are you—"

"Silence!" she shouted, slamming her fist down on her desk like an auctioneer's gavel. "Scarlet's place needs to be filled, and it is fortuitous that we have someone to fill it. We shall not have the good name of Rookwood School tarnished by unfortunate circumstances. We've put the absence before summer down to a bout of influenza, which you, *Scarlet*," she looked at me pointedly, "have recovered from well."

I was lost, reeling, and the room span around me. Perhaps this was a nightmare, and in reality I was in a tormented sleep back at my aunt's house.

"But..." I protested. "You didn't accept me for the scholarship! Only Scarlet passed the entrance exam." I had never forgiven myself for that. I'd been up all of the previous night fretting about it, and I was sure I hadn't studied enough.

"That is irrelevant, child. The fees are already paid. You will take your sister's place for the sake of the greater good. From now on, *you are Scarlet*. Ivy might not have passed the entrance exam, but *you* did."

I wanted to shout at her, but my lips were quivering and my breathing was shallow and panicked. "P-please, why do I have to do this?"

She held out a finger to silence me, the tip of her nail long and sharp.

"It does not concern you. These are adult matters, and we shall deal with them as we see fit. You don't want to trouble the other pupils with this, do you?" She leant back and looked away from me.

"D-does my father know about this, Miss?" If everyone at the school was clueless, I hoped there was a chance that Father had been deceived as well.

My hopes were shattered when she replied, "Of course he does. We have his full permission. *He* understands that it's the best way. Now," she continued, "we've kept your room for you. Breakfast is at seven thirty." She started tapping her fountain pen, and talking in a flat voice as though she were reading from an invisible blackboard. "Lessons start at nine." *Tap*. "The matron's office is at the end of our corridor." *Tap*. "No loitering in the hallways." *Tap tap*. "Lights out at nine o'clock..."

I should have been listening to the rules, but I couldn't help being distracted by the items on Miss Fox's desk – a lamp, a telephone, an inkwell, an ivory paperweight, a chequebook, a small golden pill-box and – oh no – a stuffed Chihuahua with a mouth full of pens.

"Pay attention, girl!"

My eyes darted back up. "Yes, Miss Fox," I replied.

Miss Fox gave an exasperated sigh. "Here, take this –" she handed me a map and a list of the school rules. "Remember, you are Scarlet now. There is no more Ivy."

She got up from the chair quickly, and waved at me to follow her.

It's quite a thing to be told that you don't exist any more. It took me a moment to stand, my legs were shaking so much.

I felt like one of the sad dogs on Miss Fox's walls. Their glassy gazes penetrated my back as I walked out of the office, trying to leave Ivy Grey behind.

*

I trailed after Miss Fox, along the corridors and up some dark, claustrophobic stairs to the first floor. The walls were lined with regimental rows of little green doors with numbers pinned on. We stopped at one bearing the number thirteen. *Of course*, Scarlet's favourite number. She laughed in the face of bad luck.

Miss Fox unlocked the door, thrust the labelled key back into the depths of her dress and left me standing in the corridor with nothing but a "get changed, girl" over her shoulder. The door was left swinging uncertainly on its hinges, and I peered inside with trepidation.

The dorm room was not unlike our bedroom at home, with two iron beds standing side by side.

In my mind, I saw Scarlet dashing in, bouncing on the mattress and untucking the bed sheets – she always said it made her feel like she was in a sarcophagus if they were too tight. She would blow a dark lock of hair from her eyes and tell me to stop looking so gormless and bring in our bags.

I stared down at my feet. There was just the one bag there, its sides slumping on the hard wooden floor.

Shaking my head, I picked it up and walked into the room, the ghost of Scarlet evaporating from my mind. I had to calm down, to pull myself together.

Sort out your room. Unpack your things. Don't forget to breathe!

Out of habit, I immediately went for the bed on the left, before realising that Scarlet would have gone for the right. I had no idea if anyone would notice such things, but I dutifully crossed to the other bed, set down my bag and looked around.

The whitewashed room contained a big oak wardrobe, a wobbly chest of drawers and a dressing table with a chipped mirror. I caught sight of myself in it. Scarlet and I had the same dark hair, same pale skin, same small features like a child's doll. Only on her it had always seemed pretty. It just made me look lost and sad.

"Scarlet," I whispered. I stepped forward and held my hand out towards the mirror. When we were younger we used to stand either side of the downstairs windows and copy each other's movements, pretending to be reflections. I would always do it backwards by accident, and she would collapse in fits of laughter. Yet now, as I waved my hand at the mirror, the image in the glass followed it exactly.

My head hurt.

In one corner of the room there was a washbasin with a sink and plain porcelain jug, with white flannels laid out next to it. Even though this room had belonged to Scarlet in the previous year, there was no sign of her.

I began to wonder what they had done with all her possessions. If they weren't here, where were they? Where were her clothes and her books? Where was...

Her diary.

When we were little, she always showed me the contents of her diary. Sometimes she would let me write in it too. A new one every year. She would fill it with drawings of us, identical stick figures living in a gingerbread cottage with the evil stepmother. But as we got older she became more secretive, always hiding it. Not that I would have read it. If there were thoughts in there that she couldn't share with me, her twin, I didn't want to know them.

Scarlet's precious diary could have been destroyed or lost or tossed away by a maid, and that thought made me shudder. But there was a small chance that Scarlet had hidden it too well for it to be found.

And if it was still here – all that was left of my sister – I desperately wanted it.

The wardrobe, I thought. It was always one of her favoured hiding places. I dashed over and flung its doors wide open, coughing at the musty smell of mothballs.

The only thing it contained was a single uniform, neatly folded over a hanger – a white long-sleeved blouse, a black pleated dress and a purple striped tie with the Rookwood crest on the end and a pair of matching stockings tucked underneath. I held the uniform up against me; it was exactly my size.

Scarlet's uniform.

I stood still for a few moments. I was being foolish. They were only clothes. Scarlet and I shared clothes all the time. But now she was gone, and it wasn't Scarlet's uniform any more, it was mine. And that scared me.

I carefully laid out the uniform on the opposite bed and continued my search. The base of the wardrobe was lined with old newspaper and I peeled up the yellowing sheets, my nose wrinkling.

Nothing.

I stood on tiptoe and felt around on the top shelf – yet more nothing, unless you counted the dust.

I tried tugging at each of the drawers of the chest in turn. Several of them stuck and I held my breath, willing the diary to be inside. But each time I managed to get one open, I was faced with an empty drawer. Scarlet's belongings may have been worthless to the school, but they weren't to me. I knew that Scarlet had our mother's silver-backed hairbrush – engraved with her initials, E.G. – as I had her pearls. Where could that be?

I fell on to my hands and knees and peered beneath the beds, but all I could see was an expanse of threadbare carpet. I tried picking at threads to see if it would come loose, hoping for a secret compartment under the floorboards, but it was well stuck down. Useless. I felt like crying.

I stood up and went over to the bed and threw myself down on to the uncomfortable mattress. Scarlet could have hidden her diary anywhere. Or maybe it had already been found, and destroyed...

Then – wait – I could feel something. There was a peculiar lump in the mattress. It was something hard and pointy. I shuffled my weight around, hoping that I wasn't imagining it. No, there was definitely something there.

I jumped up, ran to the door and checked the corridor for teachers. It was silent, empty. I prayed that Miss Fox wouldn't return any time soon.

Certain that no one was coming, I pulled off the grey blankets and bed sheets, throwing them into a heap on the floor. I ran my hand over the bare mattress, and I could still feel the lump. But there was no way to get to it. Or was there?

I got down on the floor and lay on my back, pulling myself right under the bed until I could see through the metal slats. It was dusty, and I had to resist a strong urge to sneeze.

And then I saw the hole. It was a long narrow slit cut into the material, maybe with a knife. *The perfect size for a diary.*

I pushed my hand into the mattress. Feathers and pieces of cotton stuffing scattered around my head and tickled my eyes as the coiled springs scraped against my skin. Then I could feel something else! It was hard and worn, maybe leather, and the tips of my fingers were just touching it.

My hand sunk in further, and I ignored the dust, the scraping, until...

There it was. I wrenched it out by the corner, and I clutched the little book to my chest, my heart pounding beneath it.

Scarlet's diary.

They hadn't found it. There was a piece of my sister waiting for me after all.

I wriggled my way out from under the bed and hastily tried in vain to brush myself off. Then I sat up, leaning against the cold frame, and stared at the book in my hands. It was brown and shiny, and the letters 'SG' had been carefully scored into the cover.

It looked as though half the pages had been torn out, but some of it was still intact. Hardly daring to breathe, I undid the leather strap, and turned to the first page that remained:

Ivy, I pray that it's you reading this.
And if you are, well, I suppose you're the new me...

Chapter Five

You must keep this a secret from <u>everyone</u>. Especially Miss Fox. She cannot hear about this, understand? I've had to split up the pages. She would do anything to destroy the evidence.

You will be fine, as long as you remember me. It's just acting, like we always said we would do. Only you'll be playing my part.

Don't pay too much attention in class. Don't wear your uniform too neatly. Stay away from Penny. Don't get on the wrong side of the Fox... you don't know what she's capable of. Don't be as <u>wet</u> as you usually are — just look in the <u>mirror</u>, remember you're *trying to be me.*

And Ivy, I give you full permission to read my diary – in fact, you MUST!

I stuffed the diary into my pillowcase, my heart racing. This was madness.

How could Scarlet possibly have known this would happen? She'd said I had to go along with the deception, and it seemed I had no choice but to do as she said. I shuddered at the thought of disobeying Miss Fox, too.

I couldn't believe the web of lies I'd found myself in. All to escape shame for the school, to stop the other pupils from panicking about the 'unfortunate circumstances'.

Who could I turn to?

Aunt Phoebe.

Of course! I ran to my bag and pulled out a pen, paper and ink. I flattened out the sheet on the dressing table and hastily scrawled:

Dear Aunt Phoebe,

Help! This has all been a huge mistake. I don't know what's going on here but they want me to pretend to be Scarlet. This can't be right. I've found her diary, and somehow she knew this would happen. Something terrible is going on here.

Could you come and get me? Or tell Father? Please, this is important!

Ivy

I folded the letter into an envelope and wrote Aunt Phoebe's address and URGENT in big letters.

But then, almost immediately, my excitement began to fade. How exactly was I going to send a letter? I didn't have a stamp, nor did I know where to find a post office. If pupils needed to send letters from the school, they probably had to give them to a teacher. And if Miss Fox got hold of it, well...

That was a chance I couldn't take. I had to trust Scarlet's words. They were all I had left.

I forced myself to change into her uniform. The fabric was scratchy and didn't smell like her at all. I looked in the mirror, but something was wrong... I loosened the tie, tugged on the hem of the dress and pulled the stockings up unevenly – there, not too neat.

Once I was dressed, I unpacked my few possessions before remaking Scarlet's – *my* – bed, and finally collapsed on it, exhausted. But as my eyelids began to drift shut, I noticed a shadow fall across the room.

"Hello," said the shadow.

I looked up. The girl barely filled the doorway. She was

small and so mousy that she looked like she might beg for cheese at any moment.

I was about to offer an equally timid "hello" in reply, but then I remembered. I had to be Scarlet now...

"Hello!" I said, jumping up from the bed and forcing a cheery smile on to my face.

The mousy girl took a small step backwards. "Um, good afternoon. MynameisAriadneI'mnew."

"Sorry?"

The girl inhaled a long, deep breath. "My name is Ariadne. Ariadne Elizabeth Gwendolyn Flitworth."

"Oh... um, sorry," I said, wincing.

"It's okay, I'm used to it," Ariadne sighed. She held out a small hand, nails bitten to extinction.

I looked at it for a second, and then shook it with nervous enthusiasm. "My name is Iv— Scarlet. Nice to meet you." *Oh dear*, I thought, as I unhooked my hand from hers. *I'm not very good at this.*

Ariadne stooped to pick up her luggage, a little convoy of suitcases trailing after her. I watched her pick up each one and gingerly lift it over to her side of the room. I didn't think to offer any help. It seemed like some kind of strange ritual.

"Are you new as well?" Ariadne suddenly asked.

"Me? Oh no," I replied, my mind racing. "I was here last year."

Ariadne looked around the bare room curiously, so I babbled on.

"Well, I was quite ill for a while. Some kind of flu, they said. Had to take all my things back home. They, erm, didn't want everyone else to catch it."

"Oh, of course," said Ariadne, tucking strands of mousy hair behind her ears as she shuffled back and forth. "My father decided to send me here, because he had to go away on important business." She didn't say this in a proud or boastful way – more like repeating something she had heard many times. She finished laying out her suitcases and turned to face me, blowing a stray hair out of her face. "Um, I don't suppose you could show me where the lavatories are?"

Oh good grief. I could hardly say that I had forgotten where the lavatories were. I hadn't even looked at the map yet and I couldn't remember seeing any signs on my way through the school either, but surely there would be some on this floor.

Ariadne was still staring at me so I quickly said, "Of course, they're just... down here," and motioned for her to go out into the corridor. As I followed, I glanced back at the bed, checking that the diary was fully concealed in my pillowcase.

Classes must have finished for the day as uniformed girls were milling about in the corridor. As I walked along, Ariadne trailing behind me, the whispers started. There were sideways glances and staring eyes and hands over mouths.

Oh, Scarlet, I thought. *What have you been up to here?*

The gauntlet seemed to stretch forever. I quickened my pace, and I heard Ariadne's rushing footsteps as she tried to keep up.

Finally, I came to a door marked 'Lavatories and Bathrooms'. "In here," I said to Ariadne, holding the door open. Then I ducked in behind her, and shut the world out.

Ariadne walked into a stall and pulled the door closed. I could still hear the commotion from outside, but it was muffled as if it were far away. I leant against the wall, trying to conceal my panic.

The lavatories were cold, with giant windows of dappled glass that let in weak light. The walls were a horrible mint green, and the paint was flaking with damp. But it was still luxury compared to Aunt Phoebe's outdoor privy and tin bath.

I went over to the sinks and wrenched at a tap, hoping to rinse some of the embarrassment off my face. At first there was nothing, then a tiny dribble. I wrenched harder, and a torrent of water shot out, splashing my dress.

Brilliant. Just brilliant.

"Scarlet?" the sound of Ariadne's voice drifted over the wooden door.

I was concentrating on wringing out my uniform and

almost didn't reply. "Ah – yes?"

"What were those girls staring at?"

I tried to imagine what Scarlet could have done to elicit such a reaction, but it could have been anything. Even her best behaviour was probably too outrageous for this school.

Before I had a chance to answer I heard the lavatory flush and the bolt of the door slide back. Ariadne appeared at the sink next to me and began washing her hands.

"Do you think they were staring at me?" she said, looking flustered. "It's because I'm new, isn't it? They probably think I'm strange, or ugly, or dull, or... or... all of those things!" She sunk down onto the floor in a heap, her dress billowing out over her legs.

I almost laughed with relief. "Actually I think they were probably staring at me. Because... because I was away for so long. They probably thought I ran away to join the circus."

"Are you sure?" she said, blinking up at me.

I wasn't sure of anything. "Absolutely. They probably didn't even notice you were there."

I suddenly realised that what I had said might have been a little insulting. But Ariadne was standing up, a quivering smile spreading across her face.

"You're right. Of course you're right." She looked at me expectantly, as if to say 'what next?'.

I didn't want to go back into the corridor again, but

we couldn't stay in the lavatories forever. So I took a deep breath and walked out. The crowds had thinned a little, but heads still turned to look at us as we passed. I sped up again, hoping that I wouldn't lose Ariadne in the throng.

When we got back to room thirteen I breathed a sigh of relief and retreated to my bed. I felt for the reassuring lump of the diary inside the pillowcase. I would have to hide it back inside the mattress as soon as possible.

Ariadne began methodically pulling items from her many suitcases. Dresses, skirts, blouses. Each item of clothing was already perfectly folded, yet she spread everything out and folded it back up again. It was oddly relaxing, watching Ariadne unpack. I enjoyed the moment of quiet.

"Well, look what the Fox dragged in."

I looked up.

A girl stood in the doorway. She had curled copper hair, a pale blue hair bow and a face full of freckles. The face might have been pretty, were it not wearing a scowl.

So much for quiet.

Ariadne walked over to her and held out a hand. "Hello!" she said. "I'm Ariadne. I'm new."

The girl completely ignored her and carried on glaring at me. "They shouldn't have let you back in, you know. You don't deserve to be here."

I stared blankly at her and then I went for the first reply

that popped into my head.

"Why?"

"Don't try and pull the innocent act on me, Scarlet Grey. We all know what you did."

"We... we do?" I asked.

"Ugh. You make me sick," she spat.

"What's your name?" piped up Ariadne.

The girl blinked at her. "What? Oh. Penny, short for Penelope."

"My name's Ariadne. It's not short for anything. It's Greek. She helped Theseus defeat the Minotaur!" She stabbed the air with her arm. "Pleased to meet you!"

Ariadne was clearly trying to make up for her earlier shyness. I wasn't sure that this was quite the way to do it.

"I'm sure you are." Penny narrowed her freckle-rimmed eyes. "Anyway. Some of us have *friends* to go and talk to." She turned on her heel and started to stalk out of the room.

"If they're friends with you, I probably don't want to talk to them," I said without thinking.

Ariadne was staring at me, open-mouthed.

That was *not* a very Ivy thing to say. In fact, it was a very *Scarlet* thing to say. A strange mix of unease and pride crept over me.

Penny leant back into the room. "You'd better be careful around her, Ariadne," she hissed. "You never know how you might end up..." She slid a finger across her throat ominously and then stalked away.

"What was *that* about?" asked Ariadne.

"I wish I knew," I said.

But, to be honest, I wasn't sure if I wanted to know at all.

Chapter Six

At six o'clock it was time for dinner. I had spent an hour listening to Ariadne telling me about her beloved pony, Oswald, and her dog, and her chickens. The whole time I was becoming more and more aware that I hadn't had anything to eat since breakfast. I would have to go down and find food, but that meant facing more people who knew Scarlet. Surely they would see through my pretence?

I left the room with Ariadne chattering away behind me. There was no need to worry about where the dining hall was

– all I had to do was follow the stream of girls flowing down the stairs. I tried to disappear, to not to think about their staring eyes.

"...and we've got this huge duck pond full of fish, you know, really really huge. It even has a bridge across it."

"Do you have any brothers and sisters?" I asked, turning to look at her as we walked.

Ariadne blinked, her train of conversation derailed. "No. It's just me and Mummy. And Daddy, sometimes. I wish I did, though. What about you?"

"Um, yes. I have a sister. But she... goes to another school. And some brothers, I suppose. Stepbrothers, really."

Ariadne sighed. "How lovely."

"You haven't met them," I said.

The dining hall was an enormous noisy room with rows of tables, all filled with girls. There was a long hatch in the wall that looked into the kitchen, and through it the cooks were spooning steaming food on to plates. Whatever the food was, the whole room smelt strongly of stew. Ariadne and I joined the back of the dinner queue. I'd never seen so many people in one place.

Everyone was talking at once, and the air was filled with the sounds of knives scraping and glasses clinking. I wanted to clamp my hands over my ears to block it all out.

Then I spotted Miss Fox, who looked very much like she wanted to do the same. She was standing at the far end of the hall, tapping a wooden cane against the side of her leg. I swallowed, uneasily.

I took a tray and a cheap-looking china plate from the pile. One of the cooks, her hair messily poking out of a white cap, lifted her ladle and spooned a large pile of gloopy brown stuff on to the plate.

"Sorry, what is it, please?" I asked.

"Stew," she replied, flatly.

"What kind of stew, Miss?"

The cook just stared at me and then turned to serve Ariadne.

As I headed into the middle of the room, I stopped and froze, realising I didn't have a clue where I was supposed to sit. But then, out of the corner of my eye, I swore Miss Fox pointed with a barely noticeable flick of the cane. Empty seats.

Ariadne followed me to the table and we sat down. She poked her food around the plate with a fork, apparently trying to make sure it was dead.

"Welcome back, Scarlet!"

I looked up. I was being addressed by a woman with greying hair and big grey eyes to match.

"Um, thank you, Miss," I responded. I scooped up some

of the stew with my fork. It wasn't as bad as it looked, but *ow*, it was hot. I swallowed it quickly.

"Decided we like the stew now, have we?" said the teacher sitting opposite us.

I stared down at my plate. "Oh. I guess it's not that bad... really?"

She smiled archly. "Indeed. Well, I always like to see a healthy appetite."

Ariadne came to my rescue. "What's your name, Miss?" she asked.

"Ah, you must be the new student! I'm Mrs Knight. I'm the head of Richmond House."

"I'm Ariadne, Miss. Pleased to meet you." She held out her hand. It still had a fork in it.

Mrs Knight ignored it, but I heard giggles rippling away from us along the table. I felt my cheeks turn red.

It wasn't long before they faded, but I noticed that one person laughed for a little longer than anyone else. I peered down the length of the table, and wasn't surprised to see Penny looking back. She gave me a fake smile, and waved her fork in my direction. Then she pretended to stab herself with it, and started making gagging noises. Her friends were in fits.

I flushed even harder. Scarlet would've done something. Perhaps she would have tipped the stew down the front of

Penny's black dress. The threat of Miss Fox's cane would mean nothing to her.

But I wasn't Scarlet. I was still Ivy. I finished my dinner in silence.

It was lights out. I lay in my nightgown, feeling strange in my new surroundings. I waited in vain for Ariadne to go to sleep. She had been whispering excitedly for the past half an hour, while I occasionally replied with 'mmmhmm' as loudly as I dared.

Once she dozed off I would be able to take out the diary. The light of the full moon through the thin curtains ought to be enough for me to read by.

"Isn't this exciting?!" Ariadne somehow managed to pronounce extra punctuation marks even when whispering.

"Shouldn't we go to sleep now?"

"But it's like a sleepover, isn't it? We can stay up all night and have a midnight feast!"

"We don't have any food, Ariadne."

"Oh, right."

I watched as she picked up a teddy from the floor. It was fluffy and bright-eyed, clearly brand new.

"I suppose I shall try and go to sleep then," she sighed, placing the teddy next to her head on the pillow and patting it gently. "I'm sure it will be absolutely *impossible*.

Goodnight, Scarlet."

"G'night," I mumbled.

She flopped down with her eyes wide open. "Impossible!" she whispered.

Exactly two minutes later, she was snoring contentedly.

Finally! I pulled the lumpy pillow from under my head. With a quick shake, the diary fell out into my lap and I turned my back to Ariadne.

I hoped the diary might hold answers, but when I opened it again I realised that it was empty aside from the letter to me. There were only torn edges of pages that had been ripped out. Where had a year of Scarlet's life gone?

I looked at the words on that remaining page again, read them over and over, the ink swimming in front of my eyes. I shook my head. *Don't be as wet as you usually are, Ivy.*

I would have fallen asleep clutching the little leather book in my arms, but I couldn't risk it. So I hid it away, and held on to the memory of my sister instead.

The following day was a Saturday; a blessing that saved me from lessons and wearing Scarlet's uniform. Ariadne and I returned to the dining hall and ate cold porridge for breakfast. It was lumpy and required far more chewing than it ought to have done.

"What shall we do today?" Ariadne asked.

I blinked up at her. What was there to do at this school?

Luckily, she didn't wait for me to respond. "I'd like to visit the library," she said. "I've heard they have a wonderful collection."

So, after a sneaky look at my map in the lavatory cubicle, we took a trip to the school library. It was an impressive sight – rows and rows of enormous shelves, stretching up to a high vaulted ceiling. There were ladders on wheels for reaching the upper levels, and some girls were laughing as they pushed each other along the racks. In the centre lay numerous tables, packed with students being studious, or at least doing a good job of pretending.

And *books*. There had to be hundreds, no, *thousands* of them. So many stories, unread. So much to learn.

Of course, I had to pretend I was completely unimpressed. Scarlet would have seen the library many times before, and she wasn't particularly interested in books.

"I'll just get... a couple out," I said to Ariadne, trying to sound bored.

"A couple? I'm going to get the maximum!" she exclaimed.

And that was how we returned to our room, me carrying a meagre two books and Ariadne tottering under an enormous pile of them. If the girls hadn't been laughing at her yesterday, they certainly were now.

*

On Sunday we had to go the school chapel for a service. The sermon echoed off the walls, but I wasn't really paying attention. I saw Scarlet everywhere, in the brass of the candles, in the stained-glass windows and in the tarnished gold collection plates. I felt like somehow she was watching me.

It started to drizzle as we filed out under the glare of Miss Fox. I tried to hurry back through the jostling crowds with Ariadne trailing behind me. But then I checked myself. *You're trying to be Scarlet – don't be so wet.*

Father had always said that she walked around like she owned the place, like there was a pole down the back of her dress. So that was what I had to do.

And it worked! The stream of girls began to move out of my way as I climbed the steps of the school. I turned back to Ariadne and smiled at her. She stopped and waved back, almost getting trampled in the process.

That was a bit more like it, wasn't it, Scarlet?

That night, accompanied by Ariadne's gentle snoring, I took out the diary, just to hold it. But I soon found myself reading the words again.

Scarlet's last line, that oft-heard insult – '*don't be as wet as you usually are – just look in the mirror*' – had been playing on my mind. It seemed out of place somehow. And why would Scarlet underline it? Unless…

What if it's one of Scarlet's secret messages that used to drive me mad? What if she's telling me to look for something? She said she'd try to leave me with some advice – did that mean this was a clue?

I looked at the underlined words again – first, something wet. A lake? A river? That seemed unlikely. And second, somewhere with mirrors…

The bathrooms.

It jumped into my head as if Scarlet had whispered it right in my ear.

It was lights out, and everyone was in bed. There was a good chance that Miss Fox would be patrolling the corridors, looking for rule-breakers. Then again, surely needing the lavatory was a valid excuse to be up in the night. I sat up in bed and looked down at my shoes. Too noisy; I'd have to go barefoot.

I tiptoed to the door – my ballet training was certainly useful for something. I had to tug on the handle hard and it made a squeaking noise as it opened that was like a scream in my head. I winced as I stuck my head out and surveyed the corridor. Empty. The nearby door marked 'Matron' was shut tight.

I hurried towards the bathrooms. Every time I passed

a door, I half expected Miss Fox to leap out from behind it. Suddenly there was a bang from the other end of the corridor, and I almost jumped out of my nightgown. It was only a window, left hanging open in the breeze.

There was a dim light in the lavatories, but through the door marked 'Bathrooms' it was a different story. I could just make out a small row of doors along the dark corridor, each with a number on it.

My heart beat faster as I tried the handle of the first door.

Inside was an enormous cast-iron bath, rusting at the edges, a flat-framed mirror and a faint smell of mildew.

I pictured Scarlet walking into the room, walking right through me. I pictured her when we were five, climbing into the bath and splashing me with soapy water. Then I pictured her sneaking in here to hide something in the last days of her life.

"What am I even looking for, Scarlet?" I whispered. There was a lump rising in my throat.

I walked to the mirror, ran my fingers over the cold glass. My reflection stared back at me, and I had to look away. I tugged on the mirror, wondering if there was anything behind it, but it was screwed tightly to the wall.

I looked around the chilly room. The pages obviously couldn't be in the bath. They certainly weren't next to it. That left only one place – underneath.

I crouched down and felt along the rough iron surface...

Nothing. My heart sank faster than the *Titanic*.

But then – I could almost hear Scarlet's laughter ringing out in my head – there were four more bathrooms to choose from, weren't there?

Two and three were as empty as number one. I shivered in my nightgown.

As I walked into number four, I thought I heard a muffled noise, somewhere nearby. I stood stock-still and listened, but there was no sound apart from the dripping of a tap. It must have been a mouse. These old buildings were full of them.

That gave me a thought. Where do mice live? Holes. Holes in the skirting, holes in the floorboards. *Hiding places*.

I crouched down and I crawled around to where the pipes descended through the floorboards. There was a jagged gap surrounding the lead pipes, just large enough to fit my fingers through.

I touched something. *Paper*.

"Oh my goodness!" I whispered, drawing it out. My hands were shaking. The pages were crumpled and covered with dust, but Scarlet's flowing handwriting was clearly visible on them.

It was then that I heard the noise again, even closer than before. I had to get back to my room as soon as possible. I walked out of the bathroom and pulled the door to behind me, as quietly as I could. And then I turned to go back into the lavatories.

Only someone was in my way.

"Hello, Scarlet," Penny said, grinning and showing her pointy teeth. "What do you think you're doing in here at this hour?"

I was right about there being a mouse. *I was the mouse.*

And Penny was the cat about to eat me alive.

Chapter Seven

Benny glared at me. "I said, 'what are you doing in here?'"

I scrunched the diary pages tightly in my fist behind my back. "I'm... it's... nothing. I just needed to go to the lavatory, that's all."

"You're up to something," she said, leaning towards me. "It's after lights out and you've been creeping around in the bathrooms. I've a good mind to tell the matron. Or how about Miss Fox?"

She stood there, arms folded, eyes narrowed.

"But," I said, my mind racing to keep up with my mouth, "won't you get into trouble as well? You're not supposed to be up either." There was a flicker of doubt in her expression. "Why don't we just go back to our rooms?"

Suddenly, she grabbed my arm and pulled it out in front of me. "Listen, you little worm," she hissed. "This is my school, and you can't sweet talk your way out of everything, understand?"

I could barely breathe. I was praying that she didn't grab my other arm as well.

Thankfully, Penny didn't seem to notice. "You think you can just walk back in here and get away with everything again, don't you?" she said.

"D-do I?" I stuttered.

"What was that?" she said, her grip tightening.

It was taking all my strength not to panic and cry. Scarlet would be tugging out a lock of Penny's copper hair or kicking her hard in the shins. I thought that wouldn't exactly be the smartest thing to do, though. Penny had the look of someone who would scream like a banshee, and I didn't want the teachers to come running.

Instead, I decided to try reason. "Penny, let's just... forget about it, all right? Whatever I did, I—"

"You know what you did," she interrupted, digging her nails into my wrist.

I gritted my teeth. "Well... I'm sorry about it. Now, can you *please* let me go, before we both get a caning?"

Her glaring eyes bore into me. "Sorry? That's all you can say?"

I blinked at her.

"Fine," she said, her voice turning strangely calm. "But you're not forgiven. And when I find out what you're up to this time, it won't be a secret for long."

I watched Penny stalk out of the room. A full minute later, I allowed myself to breathe a sigh of relief, and brought my fist holding the diary pages shakily in front of me again.

What a nightmare.

I went back down the dark corridor as silently as I could, and prised open door number thirteen. Ariadne was asleep with her pillow over her head. Good.

I folded the thin cotton sheets and the blankets back over myself and flattened out the new pages against the wall.

You're going to meet a girl named Penny Winchester. She's got a whole swarm of bees in her bonnet when it comes to me, so you should <u>STAY AWAY FROM HER</u>.

That was Scarlet – always late.

Penny thinks she's the queen, and will try and order you about *so you have to put her in her place. She actually has more in common with a poisonous toad.*

I smiled for the first time in what felt like days.

The other person you have to watch out for is Nadia Sayani. She's shaping up to be Penny's new sidekick. She looks pretty and simple but don't be fooled; she's super rich and super clever, so you'll have to brush up on your acting skills. She might spot that something's afoot.

I wasn't sure if I was capable of acting anything *but* suspicious.

Now, you need to find the rest of my diary. You CANNOT let anyone else see it. But someone needs to know the truth about

About what?

I looked around frantically. Had I dropped the next page somewhere?

No, I couldn't have. They were scrunched up so tightly in my hand that I had almost lost the feeling in it.

So what was the next clue? Scarlet was probably up there laughing at me, calling me a dunce for not knowing the *obvious* place she had hidden the other pages.

The truth about what?

I gently tucked the pages inside the leather cover of the diary, and got down on all fours to hide it back inside the mattress, and then I climbed into bed.

A delicate snore came from Ariadne's side, and reminded me that it was getting late. Tomorrow was another day. Another day of doing a bad impersonation of my twin. Another day spent fearing that someone would catch me out at any moment.

Another day without Scarlet.

I pulled my pillow over my head, and tried my hardest to go to sleep, as Scarlet's final words danced across my mind.

On Monday we were woken at seven by a shrill bell. I sat there at breakfast, feeling uncomfortable in Scarlet's uniform, as Mrs Knight babbled away about something to do with her rhododendrons. Penny wasn't looking at me. I hoped that she was keeping quiet about last night.

We had an assembly, where we sang hymns and listened to Miss Fox drone on about the school rules. She obviously liked rules much more than she liked people. There seemed to be hundreds, and I wondered how I was ever going to remember them all.

Our first lesson was history and luckily Ariadne had spent yesterday memorising our timetable and the classroom map, so I was able to follow her to class.

"Are you good at history, Scarlet?" she asked me as we walked. "It's my favourite."

Scarlet was useless at history. I, on the other hand, had a great memory for names and dates. "It's all right, I suppose," I said feebly.

"My great-great-granddaddy fought against Napoleon, you know," replied Ariadne.

I feigned polite interest, but as we walked through the echoing corridors all I could think about was how to keep up this act in front of Scarlet's teachers. Surely they would notice that I wasn't my sister?

We joined a line of girls outside the classroom and filed in silently. I suddenly realised, too late, that I had no idea which desk belonged to Scarlet.

I felt like a bird in a flock that had just flown the wrong way. Which seat should I choose?

"What's the matter, Scarlet?" said a simpering voice that could only belong to Penny. "Did you leave your brain at home?"

Giggles flooded the room as my cheeks heated up. At that moment there was a thud and a giant cloud of white dust billowed out of a cupboard.

From the cloud of dust emerged a coughing, white-haired woman. She waved her hand frantically, trying to disperse it.

We all stared as she coughed for what felt like an age, and then finally slammed her blackboard rubbers down on her desk and pointed a quivering finger at me.

"Scarlet Grey!" she said, in an accusatory tone.

"Yes, Miss?" I responded, trying to hide the fear in my voice.

"That's Madame Lovelace to you, insolent girl!" She pronounced it *Loveless*. "Why aren't you at your desk?"

"I-I fancied a change of scenery?"

I heard snickers from behind me.

Madame Lovelace glared. "And you," she said. "Who are you?"

Hang on a minute. Who was she talking to? I turned around and saw Ariadne standing just behind me, looking sheepish.

"Um," said Ariadne. "I'm new."

Madame Lovelace gave an exaggerated sigh. "Both of you, sit down," she said, jabbing her finger in the direction of two unoccupied desks in the first row.

Relieved, I hurried to the nearest one and sat down.

"Now, girls," said the teacher, slapping at her dusty dress. "Open your desks and take out your pens, please. Today we shall be studying the Battle of Waterloo."

The lid of my desk was woodworm-speckled and decorated with a little brass number four, plus many years of idle scratches. I lifted it up. It smelt of ink and paper inside, and a familiar floral scent that went straight to my heart.

Scarlet. It was the rose perfume that she'd worn for the past few years after getting a bottle of it for Christmas.

I glanced around the class to see if anyone else had noticed the smell, but the other students looked half asleep. Madame Lovelace began to dictate lines about Napoleon and the Duke of Wellington.

Ariadne put her hand up. "My great-great-granddaddy fought against Napoleon," she said.

"Very nice, dear," said Madame Lovelace, looking displeased at the interruption.

I peered into the desk. There was a book in the bottom, with *The History of Great Britain* written in dull, heavy letters on the cover. I took it out.

"Now," said Madame Lovelace, "turn to page fifty-three for a list of the important historical figures involved in the battle. Make a note of these, as you will need to remember them." She punctuated every sentence with occasional coughs.

I heard Penny giggle quietly behind me.

I opened up the book and the smell of Scarlet's perfume hit me so strongly I almost choked. It was as though she'd poured it all over the pages. I looked at Ariadne. Even she was wrinkling her mousey nose, so I slammed the cover shut.

"Miss Grey!" shouted Madame Lovelace.

"Yes?"

"Yes *Madame*. Do you have a problem with your book?"

"No, Madame."

"Then kindly stop abusing it and pay attention!"

For the rest of the lesson I tried to ignore the perfume, but it felt like it was seeping into my mind. Why would Scarlet have brought her precious bottle into class?

At ten o'clock the bell rang and everyone began to filter out of the room. I had to think of a reason to stay behind.

"Madame Lovelace?" I asked.

She peered up at me over her thick-rimmed glasses. "Yes, Miss Grey?"

"May I clean the blackboard for you?"

Madame Lovelace looked like I'd just offered to spit in her tea. "Are you up to something, girl?" she said, the corners of her eyes wrinkling as she frowned. "The Scarlet Grey I know wouldn't have cleaned my blackboard without the threat of the cane."

Oh no! She might tell Miss Fox and then... *No. Stay calm.* My mind scrambled for something to say.

"I'm turning over a new leaf." I swallowed and tried again. "I shouldn't have been insolent earlier. I thought I should make up for it."

I half expected Madame Lovelace to stand up, point her

bony finger at me and shriek that I was an imposter. Scarlet never made apologies for herself. I was always the one who had to do the apologising.

But it didn't happen. Instead, she just blinked at me a few times and then said, "Very well. Just make sure you clap the rubbers out afterwards. I do *hate* chalk dust." She gave a small cough again, and I wasn't sure whether or not she was illustrating her point. "You can have a house point for that."

I nodded, although I had no idea what a house point was, or what I did with one.

I watched her shuffle out of the room, and then lifted the heavy desk lid. Underneath where the book had lain were several old sheets of paper and a green exercise book, all of which smelt like a rose garden. And underneath that I spotted the catch. A little metal thing in the bottom. I lifted it, and it opened a smaller hole. Inside it was an ink well, some dusty old pen nibs and – folded into a tiny square – a piece of paper.

I snatched it out quickly and immediately my eyes were drawn to the first word...

her.

Her? The last line from Scarlet's diary reappeared in my mind. *Someone needs to know the truth about... her.*

The question was – *who was she?*

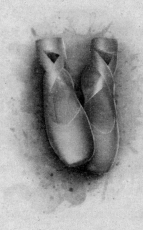

Chapter Eight

Someone needs to know the truth about her. And what's really going on at this school because otherwise the Fox will have won.

I know you can do this, Ivy. I believe in you.

Your sister,

Scarlet x

P.S. This is the final straw.

I wiped a tear from my cheek. I'd spent a good deal of my life alternately being infuriated by Scarlet or trailing after her like a lost puppy, but now I missed her more than anything.

I folded the paper neatly and hid it in my dress pocket. I sat staring into Scarlet's rose-scented desk, the silence of the empty classroom flowing around me. But then I noticed the ticking of the clock and realised that it was only two minutes until my next lesson.

I glanced up at the blackboard. It was still completely covered with names and dates! I picked up a dusty board rubber from Madame Lovelace's desk and scrubbed it as hard as I could. Chalk filled my nose and I suppressed the urge to sneeze. It was useless. I'd wiped the whole thing and it had just turned from writing to a white cloud, no black in sight. It would have to do. Madame wouldn't expect Scarlet to do a decent job of it, anyway.

I hurried out of the classroom and heard someone call out to me.

"Scarlet!"

I spun around to see Ariadne leaning up against the wall.

"Have you been there the whole time?" I said, baffled.

"I was waiting for you," she said, staring at her shoes.

Oops. I hoped she hadn't seen me looking in the desk. "Oh..."

"What were you doing in there?" she asked.

I ran a hand through my hair. "I didn't want to get on

Madame Lovelace's bad side already, so I cleaned the blackboard for her."

Ariadne looked confused and then panicked. "It must be time for home economics! It's in W3, right? The third room in the west wing?"

"Of course," I said. "Perhaps you should lead the way, so that you remember how to get there."

Ariadne nodded and then set off in what I hoped was the right direction, her little leather satchel bobbing up and down on her back. I followed behind, keeping my hand curled tightly around the diary page in my pocket.

The rest of the morning was a blur. I tried to act indifferently in my lessons, even when they were fascinating, like the stuff about Isaac Newton and gravity, or fun, like making Victoria sponges in home economics. I spent lunch ignoring the looks that Penny tried to give me. By the afternoon I felt exhausted from the effort of being Scarlet, and couldn't remember what I'd been doing most of the time. All I could think of was the letter in the diary.

And then it came to the last class of the day. Sport.

Miss Fox lined us all up in the hall and we stood there blinking in the low sunlight spilling through the windows.

"Now, girls," she said sharply, "as it's the beginning of

term, you must pick which exercise to partake in. You may choose between swimming, horse riding, hockey, lacrosse and ballet. However, if you are lacking in any particular talent –" she looked one of the larger students up and down like she was a cow at a market – "I recommend you take part in one of the team sports. I'm sure we can find a place for you somewhere in the field."

The girl hung her head even lower than it had been before. I shuffled uncomfortably, tugging at the hem of my uniform. I was glad not to be the focus of Miss Fox's attention for once.

"Write your names on the sign-up sheets and join your classes," said Miss Fox.

I thought immediately of my soft pink ballet shoes wrapped in tissue. I hadn't danced since Scarlet died. But even if I felt hesitant about starting again, there was no choice. Scarlet would have picked ballet.

So I headed straight for the corner where a group of slim, elegant girls had already gathered. But before I could get there, Miss Fox had grabbed my arm.

"I presume you'll be choosing ballet, Miss Grey?" she hissed in my ear.

I looked up at her, wide-eyed. "Yes, I'm good at ballet, Miss," I said. "I've had lessons for years."

Miss Fox gave me a nod, accompanied by a murderous stare, but before she could say anything else another teacher appeared next to us – a tall, strong-looking woman with bobbed hair – and started talking loudly about a shortage of hockey sticks.

I glanced over at the hockey corner. A group of nervous-looking girls stood there, and I was surprised to see Ariadne among them. She shrugged hopefully and I waved back. I couldn't imagine poor Ariadne lasting through five minutes of hockey but it seemed Miss Fox had struck a nerve.

I joined the ballet girls. It took me a few seconds to remind myself to write *Scarlet*, not *Ivy*. I pulled out my fountain pen and signed my name with a flourish. I prayed that no-one was paying close enough attention to notice that I wrote with my left hand, not my right.

When I looked up, the other ballet girls were all staring in my direction.

"Scarlet," said one of them. She had dark skin and big wide eyes, like a deer's. It wasn't a greeting, or a question, just a statement.

"Hello?" I said guardedly.

The other girls giggled and turned aside, whispering to each other. Several of them had already pulled their hair into tight buns, giving their faces a strange, sharp quality.

"Is this everyone?" I heard a voice say behind me.

I turned around to see a woman who looked so young that had she not been out of uniform I wouldn't have been sure if she was a pupil or a teacher. She was wearing a black leotard with a long white satin skirt and a matching headband. Her hair was red, not a wiry copper like Penny's but a lovely soft colour, almost blonde.

"Yes, Miss Finch," said the deer-eyed girl.

"Nearly the same as last year, then. You girls go and get changed, and then meet me in the studio." She smiled at me warmly. That was a relief, at least.

I trekked back up to my room to get my ballet clothes. As I stretched my pink tights over my legs, I felt like I was secretly becoming myself again.

The ballet studio was one of the few locations I remembered from the map that Miss Fox had given me, in the school's basement. Winding stairs led down to it, and I could feel the air getting colder as I descended.

The studio itself was lit with gas lamps rather than the modern electric lights I had seen dotted elsewhere in the school. It had wooden floorboards and a mirrored wall, with a *barre* running all the way around it. I winced as I caught sight of my flickering reflection. With my hair tied up I somehow looked even more like Scarlet.

Most of the others were warming up at the *barre*, doing familiar stretches. I stayed at the far end of the room, hoping to avoid anyone's attention.

I laced on my toe shoes, then began copying the rest of

them. It felt good to be doing something I understood. If only I didn't have to look at my own face quite so much. I tried to do my exercises facing away from the mirror.

A chiming note rang out around the room. Miss Finch was sitting at a shiny black grand piano in the corner. It looked new and expensive. "I'm glad to see everyone's remembered their warm-up," she said. "You're going to need it. I apologise for the temperature of the studio, but unfortunately the heating isn't wonderful down here."

Some of the other dancers were rubbing their arms, and I had goose bumps rising already.

"Anyway," she continued, "please carry on with your exercises at the *barre*."

As everyone began to practice their *pliés* and *tendus*, Miss Finch sighed and shuffled her sheet music half-heartedly. A moment later she slipped out through a door at the back of the room.

"Centre work now, girls," she said when she reappeared. We all moved into the middle of the room and began our exercises there. She walked between us, occasionally correcting arm and leg positions.

I was out of practice. My muscles ached as I stretched them, my joints clicked. At least I remembered the moves well enough.

Miss Finch instructed us to move on to *adagio*, where she

led us through different steps. I watched closely as she tried to demonstrate, and I noticed that although she was quick and graceful, her right leg seemed to be trailing. When she walked she had a limp, as if it pained her.

The room was getting warmer the more we danced in the glow of the gas lamps. The sound of our shoes shuffling on the floorboards was relaxing, especially now that the others were too busy concentrating to whisper about me. Well, about Scarlet.

Finally we came to *allegro*, the part of the class where you do the fastest steps, turns and jumps. It was always my favourite part, and despite my aching legs I was longing to try it again.

But while I was doing my pirouette, I lost my balance, and before I knew it I had hit the floor with a thump. The sounds of stifled laughter reached my ears.

I looked up to see Miss Finch standing above me.

"Really, Scarlet?" she said. "You need to move your head before you complete the turn, or you'll lose your balance and momentum. You know that."

I nodded, ashamed. I knew that full well. "Sorry, Miss Finch," I replied. I was obviously more rusty than Scarlet had been.

We concluded the class with *reverence*, where we curtsied to Miss Finch as she played some sweet, flowing music on the piano.

As she waved everyone out, I lingered behind, wanting to avoid the other girls. The deer-eyed one gave me a suspicious look under her eyebrows as she walked out.

I was trying to take as long as possible to unlace my shoes, and eventually Miss Finch noticed my presence. "Scarlet? Is something the matter? You didn't seem like yourself today."

That wasn't good. I shook my head. "It's fine, Miss. I'm just getting used to things again after being ill for such a long time."

"Well, you were a little less –" she waved her hand in the air, as if searching for the right word – "*unruly* than usual."

That sounded like Scarlet all right. "Sorry, Miss," I replied. "I'll try to be more unruly in future."

Miss Finch laughed. "It's good to have you back. None of us will miss Penny though, eh?" She turned around on her piano stool and played a trill of notes in succession.

I smiled, but I didn't have any idea what she was talking about. *What had Penny got to do with anything?* I wanted to ask, but I had to stop myself before the words rolled off my tongue. Whatever it was, Scarlet must have known about it. "Good riddance!" I said instead.

Miss Finch stood up, a little awkwardly on her bad leg. "You'd better get going now," she said. "Perhaps you and

Penny could sort out your differences, despite what happened before. Don't you think?"

I nodded, but I remained silent.

How could I sort out our differences when I didn't even know what they were?

Chapter Nine

That night I lay in the unfamiliar sheets of my new bed, wondering what had really happened between my sister and Penny.

"What did you do, Scarlet?" I whispered into my pillow. I received no answer but the sound of the wind blowing through the trees.

I read the diary pages over and over again, with fevered glances to make sure Ariadne was asleep, but I wasn't learning anything new. Still, it was comforting to read Scarlet's words by the moonlight. I could almost imagine her sitting with me, whispering them into my ear. She had always been one for riddles. I could never get the hang of them.

I hid the diary back in the mattress during the day. I hoped it was a place that no one was likely to look, even my roommate. Though I was sure if Ariadne found it, she'd presume it belonged to me and not even take a peek out of sheer niceness.

But there were more devious people to think about. *Penny. Miss Fox.* I prayed that they didn't know about the diary, and I shuddered to think of either of them getting their hands on it.

I flipped my pillow to the cold side and attempted sleep, but none came. I dreaded living another day of Scarlet's life, convinced that I was going to be found out. And if that happened, Miss Fox was sure to have me expelled and I'd never find out what Scarlet was trying to tell me.

Still, there was hope. Even if I had to search the entire school, I would find the rest of her messages.

Just tell me where to look, Scarlet.

I spent most of the next day in a sleep-deprived daze, my eyes fuzzy and bits of my curled fringe sticking out at awkward angles. Yet whenever I got the chance, I searched. I lifted up the desk lids in every classroom, peered under the tables in the dining hall, even opened up the high cisterns in the lavatories.

When Ariadne spotted me trying to get a glance under our English teacher's desk after class, I hastily told her I had lost a ring, even though wearing jewellery was forbidden at Rookwood. This resulted in Ariadne telling me a rather rambling story about how her mother thought she'd lost her wedding ring in Venice and ordered a gondolier to search the canals for it. The elusive ring was eventually located on the finger of their maid back in Shropshire, who had apparently been given it by the light-fingered stable boy.

If anything, this story was helpful because it meant that Ariadne didn't seem to find my erratic searching at all questionable.

"What does it look like?" she asked, as we got on our hands and knees to examine the floor of the classroom.

"It's... gold," I said. "With a ruby in it."

"Oh my goodness!" Ariadne exclaimed. "It must be of such value!"

"Oh, definitely." *Well, zero is a value*, I thought.

I hadn't considered what I'd do if I actually found more of the pages in front of Ariadne, but she was so keen to help me and I found her presence oddly reassuring.

In fact, I realised, as we scrabbled on the floor together, she was becoming a friend. She was the only person who was looking at me and not seeing my sister.

*

At dinner time, Ariadne was still searching for my non-existent ring, and almost got a caning for attempting to crawl under the dining table to look for it.

Penny found all this hilarious. As she leant back in her chair, pretending to stifle her laughter, I noticed the girl from ballet sitting next to her. She was laughing too, but there was suspicion in her deep brown eyes. *Nadia*, I realised. *Nadia Sayani. This is the other girl Scarlet warned me about.*

I frowned as I ate my cold ham and potatoes. I almost preferred it when they were laughing at me. As much as I loved my twin, she had surely done something to provoke them – Ariadne was as harmless as they come.

When we got back to our room that night, I made a show of looking around for 'the ring' as Ariadne watched me from her bed, a miserable expression on her face.

"I'm so sorry, Scarlet," she said. "We'll find it tomorrow, I know we will."

I felt awful for lying. My new life was just lies upon lies. And now it seemed like Ariadne would never stop worrying about my non-existent ring. "It's fine," I reassured her. "It doesn't matter if we can't find it. I'll live."

Ariadne nodded sadly and folded herself into her bed sheets. I plaited my hair and got into my own bed.

Once again my eyes refused to shut, and I lay awake with thoughts of Scarlet and Miss Fox and the diary spinning around my head.

A few days later, I walked down the dark steps to the ballet studio, bleary-eyed. I was shocked to see Miss Fox standing over the piano. She glared at us all as we walked in. Didn't she have any other expressions?

"Girls," she said. "Miss Finch is *unwell* today and won't be taking your class. Instead, you will join in the swimming lesson with Miss Bowler."

Everyone groaned. Miss Fox tapped her cane sharply against the floor. "That's quite enough! Swimming is an essential part of your education. You never know when someone will push you out of a boat." She looked pointedly at me. "Now get changed and off to the pool with you!"

The swimming pool was outdoors, as I discovered – much to my dismay – when I followed the other girls there after changing back into my uniform in my room. It was a bright day, but it definitely wasn't warm enough to submerge myself in freezing water. Nothing short of tropical conditions would make that seem welcoming.

An old stone building next to the pool had been converted into changing rooms, its outer walls lined with striped life rings. The swimming class were already lined up outside, so the rest of us joined the back of the queue. I gazed into the water and shivered. Scarlet and I splashed around in the brook during hot summers, but I had never been in a pool before. This one had a faint green colour to it and looked wholly uninviting.

A stout flustered-looking woman appeared, reflected in the murky water.

"Class, it looks like we're being joined by extra students today." Miss Bowler looked down at the wooden clipboard she was holding. "I'll take the register, and then you'll need to get changed as quickly as possible."

I didn't have a bathing suit. I started to feel panicked, before I realised that no one else from the ballet class would either.

"You girls will have to borrow one of these each," she said, leading us to a large cupboard filled with woollen bathing suits. They were saggy blue things with the Rookwood School logo embroidered over the chest. I must have spent a little too long staring at mine in revulsion, because Miss Bowler clapped her hands in front of my face and gestured dramatically towards the changing area.

I heard snickering nearby and wasn't surprised to see it was coming from Nadia. "What's wrong, Scarlet?" She was already changed, and somehow managed to make the hideous thing look glamorous.

I gave her my attempt at the angry-Scarlet look, narrowed eyes and stiff cheeks. Nadia seemed unfazed, responding with a smug expression of her own. I ignored her and tried to remove my clothes without revealing any of myself, which was quite a feat. I wriggled into the bathing suit. It was itchy, cold and smelt of mothballs.

There was a rubber swimming cap on the hook in front of me. I already had my hair up tight for ballet, so I just pulled the cap over it. I was quite sure I looked a sight.

I put my clothes into locker number twenty-four, and took out the little brown key. It was on a safety pin, which pricked at my skin when I attached it to my bathing suit, a tiny spot of blood appearing on the fabric.

We went out to the pool, and Miss Bowler lined us up, stood on a wooden box and made us follow her arm gestures.

"No, like *this*, Ethel! Straighten and bend! One in front of the other! Mary Jones, you look like a diseased frog!"

I tried my best to keep up, but the movements were unfamiliar. Not to mention that I had no idea how to translate them into actual swimming.

"Right! Time to get into the water, ladies."

I winced. My toes were already turning blue.

"Line up along the edge of the pool."

With a class twice as big as it should have been, there

was very little room. I gingerly curled my toes over the concrete edge.

Moments later I felt an elbow in my back and suddenly I was submerged in the icy pool. I thrashed my arms out desperately, my mouth and nose filling up.

The murky water closed over my head.

Chapter Ten

I truly thought I would drown. That the last thing I would see would be the bottom of Rookwood's pool. I saw distorted greeny-blue water, the bubbles from my gaping mouth lit up with waving shafts of sunlight. *Drowning.*

The day I heard the news about Scarlet, the rain was pouring down. It made me wonder, *Can you drown in the rain?* They say that you feel it when something happens to your twin, but I felt nothing. I had no idea she was gone.

The rain fell and fell.

No, I thought blinking wildly, *I want to stay alive. For Scarlet, and for me.*

I stretched out my legs and found the bottom of the pool with my toes. I launched myself back to the surface and managed to push my head above water, gasping and spluttering.

"NADIA SAYANI!" I heard Miss Bowler shout.

I blinked and wiped my eyes. Nadia was standing over me looking pleased with herself.

"She slipped, Miss, honest," she said, batting her eyelashes. A group of girls snickered behind her.

"It didn't look like that to me," Miss Bowler replied. She picked up a wooden ruler that was leaning against the wall. "Knuckles out!"

"But Miss, I..."

The swimming teacher grabbed hold of Nadia's arms and slapped the ruler across both of her hands, hard, leaving a red slash on her skin. Nadia winced, tears pricking the corner of her eyes. Meanwhile I was still trying to evict the water from my lungs. It burned in my nose and throat as I heaved in the fresh air.

"Calm down, Scarlet," ordered Miss Bowler.

I nodded and coughed simultaneously. I could feel everyone's eyes on me, with Nadia giving me an especially lethal glare. Even though she'd only been punished because she'd pushed me in the first place.

"Everyone in! I want to see ten lengths from all of you!"

When the torture of the swimming lesson was over, we headed back into the changing hut to shower in lukewarm water. I had never been in a shower before, and afterwards I didn't have much desire to do it ever again. But I was pleased to see that Nadia chose to stay as far away from me as possible. I'd had to swim alongside her, managing a passable attempt at a stroke and splashing a *little* more water in her direction than was necessary.

Miss Bowler handed me a threadbare cotton towel, which bore a faded Rookwood crest. I did my best to wrap the towel around myself, concealing my body as I peeled off the horrible woollen bathing suit. I felt as though I'd never get warm again.

I went to the locker and retrieved my clothes. Stepping back into Scarlet's uniform was strangely comforting.

"Back to your dorms, girls," said the teacher. "You have a couple of hours until dinner. And continue to work on your strokes. Especially you, Scarlet!"

"Yes, Miss," I said.

But in my head I prayed that Miss Finch would be back in time for our next ballet class. I didn't think I'd survive another swimming lesson.

I trailed behind the other girls and we walked into the hockey class coming back from the field. I wasn't surprised to see Ariadne at the back of the group. Her hockey socks were ripped in several places, there were bruises blossoming on her legs and arms, and she had a nasty lump on her forehead.

I ran over to her. "Goodness, what happened?" I asked.

She leant on my shoulder and stopped to catch her breath. "Hockey," she gasped, "is a lot more... *violent* than I realised. I got hit with... three balls, two sticks and four elbows! It was a massacre!"

She looked up and caught sight of my slightly damp hair, which hadn't been brilliantly protected by the swimming cap. "Have you been swimming?"

"Unfortunately, yes. Our ballet class was cancelled, so I had to."

Ariadne rubbed her forehead and sighed. "I think I'd rather go swimming than play hockey again. I don't know what Miss Fox was talking about, saying it was easier."

"I think she just likes to see people suffer," I said, trying to squeeze some of the water out of my hair. Ariadne nodded vigorously in agreement.

I glanced around. Everyone else had gone inside, and we were left in the courtyard. Ahead of us, Rookwood School stood, tall and imposing. To the right, some distance away from anything else, there was a long building.

"What's that?" I asked, pointing, and then fought the urge to put my fist in my mouth.

Ariadne looked at me, bemused. "I think it's the riding stables. But... you know that, don't you?"

"Oh," I said, "no, not the stables. I-I saw some kind of strange bird over there. It was really big. And blue."

"A peacock!" said Ariadne, a smile spreading across her face. "I love them! Their tails are like fabulous evening gowns."

I tried to ignore Ariadne's implication that I didn't know what a peacock was. I had a feeling there was something important I was missing.

"I might go and take a look," I said. And then, after a moment, "I like peacocks too."

Ariadne gave me a pained expression, and tried to blow a lock of mousy hair away from the bump on her head. "Well, I think... I think I need a rest," she said. "And I don't want to get covered in straw as well as bruises. Besides, I'd rather not go to the stables. It'll only make me miss Oswald."

I'd forgotten that Ariadne had a pony. I was under the impression that girls could keep their own horses at the school, yet hers wasn't here. Poor Ariadne.

I patted her gently on the back, the one place that didn't

seem to be bruised. "Why don't you head for the dorm? We can both come another day and search for peacocks. Perhaps we could find a carrot to give the horses, while we're at it."

Ariadne's mouth twitched up at the corners. "Really?"

"Well, I'm not sure if the cooks here actually know what real vegetables are, but we can try."

"Thanks, Scarlet. I'll see you upstairs."

I watched her limp over the gravel towards the main building. I walked off down the path and peered around the corner of the stable block. The place was deserted, apart from its animal inhabitants. The nearest horse turned its head curiously towards me, brown nostrils flaring. I stepped out into the little courtyard and petted it.

Something snapped under my shoes, and I looked down. I was standing in a pile of straw.

Straw...

A memory flared.

This is the final straw.

Straw. The kind of thing you might find in, oh, say a *stable*!

"Thank you, Scarlet," I murmured.

There were three rows of stalls, each with five doors. I bit my lip, trying to think. If she had hidden anything in here, it could take me an age to find it.

I stared at the brass-numbered doors and I thought

about the bathrooms, and how they'd been numbered too. I'd found the first diary entries in bathroom number four... And Scarlet's desk in Madame Lovelace's class – that was number four too!

Stall number four contained an unusually large black horse. The nameplate above the stable door read 'Raven'. He walked towards me as I came near, and I could hear his hoof scraping against the ground.

"Shh, boy," I whispered. "This is top-secret business."

The horse flicked his tail and blinked dark eyes at me. I tried shooing him to the back of the stall, but he just snorted disdainfully.

I looked around the courtyard for something to distract him.

There! Next to a stone mounting block, someone had left a crate with 'Bramley Apples' printed on the side. There was a single apple left in the bottom, looking rather sad.

Everyone else should be inside at this time of day, but I had no idea when the staff came by to check on the animals. I kept my ears pricked as I climbed on to the upturned crate and swung my leg over the stable door.

Raven snorted again and backed off.

"Just checking on things," I whispered, handing him the apple with the flat of my hand. He took it gratefully and began munching away.

It wasn't a particularly big space. The floor was covered in trampled straw, and a food and water trough lay in one corner with a hay net hanging above it. There was a strong smell of horse.

Not for the first time, I wondered if Scarlet couldn't have picked a more convenient hiding place. The next one could be at the bottom of the pool for all I knew!

That's why you're here, I reminded myself. Standing with damp hair and goose bumps in the middle of a stable.

It was unlikely that the pages would be anywhere on the floor. They'd be stood on or eaten in a day. So I turned to the walls. I felt the thick wooden slats that separated the stall from the one next door, searching for any holes or hidden panels. *Nothing*.

Raven whinnied as I went past him, dropping half of his apple to the floor. I hushed him again. "Easy, boy! Do you want me to get caught?" I hoped he would stay quiet, and hoped even more that he wouldn't get cross and start kicking. *That* could be fatal.

As I pondered this, I suddenly noticed something on the wall. There was an arrow chalked there – tiny, imperceptible, unless you were paying attention. And, as I looked, I saw that there was a slender gap at the top of the wooden wall. I stood *en pointe*, the best I could in leather school shoes, and reached up to the top. I worked my way along slowly, feeling for anything stuck up there.

I could have sworn the horse was looking at me as if I were mad.

And then, when I got to the rear of the stall, I felt the rustle of paper under my cold skin.

More pages!

I pulled them down, exhilaration rushing through my veins. Scarlet's handwriting met my eyes and I smiled. But I couldn't risk reading the words straight away where anyone might come by, so I concealed the pages in the waistband of my dress and started to make my way out of the stall.

Then Raven began to make a sort of low grumbling noise. And seconds later I heard footsteps approaching.

Oh no.

And worse, I recognised those footsteps.

The clacking sound that those shoes made on the stones.

The jangling of keys in pockets.

I looked up, and there was Miss Fox, standing in the doorway.

"*Scarlet Grey!*" she boomed. "What on *earth* are you doing in my stable?"

Chapter Eleven

Miss Fox flung open the door of the stall and pulled me out into the courtyard. "What do you think you're doing?" she hissed.

In a panic I ended up saying the first thing that came to mind. "*Your* stable?"

"Yes, *my* stable! Which you appeared to be in with *my* horse. When you should not be out here at all. Would you care to explain yourself, child?"

I opened my mouth, but there was nothing I could say and she knew it. Her dark eyes bored into me.

"I can't," I said.

Her mouth dropped open a little in shock. "Excuse me?"

"I can't, Miss. I don't have an explanation," I breathed.

She grabbed me roughly by the ear and I fought the urge to scream. "Thought you'd play a prank, did you? Steal the shoes from my horse? Maybe set him loose in the playing fields?"

I tried to pull away from her and my ear burned. I squeezed my lips shut, my eyes too. Let her think I was being a rule-breaker. Anything was better than her finding out about the diary pages wedged in my waistband.

"You horrible, insolent girl!" she screamed at me. "I will not tolerate this behaviour in my school! Do you understand?"

I winced. "Yes, Miss."

"You're no better than your good-for-nothing sister!" she hissed.

Suddenly, she let go of my ear. Had I miraculously escaped punishment? No, Miss Fox was just glancing around to make sure that no one else could have heard what she said.

She leant forward and I could feel her cold breath on my throat. "Your sister is gone," she said, so quietly that I could barely hear her, "and nobody has even noticed. Do you think anyone would miss you?"

I froze, terrified.

Then she cleared her throat, and straightened her back once more. "Come with me, *Scarlet*. Perhaps a taste of the cane will remind you how we do things in *my* school!"

Before I could blink, her talon-like nails were clinging to my arm and she was hauling me back towards the school building. My heels bit into the dirt and tears pricked at my eyes. The heavy door almost caught me on the way in, and gasps followed us down the corridors as the Fox dragged in its prey.

It was time to face my punishment.

I wasn't allowed to attend dinner that night. I was glad of it, because I didn't feel like eating. I lay in bed, too sore to move, too upset to want to. My skin was covered in bruises, and I felt dizzy and nauseous. And to top it all off, I felt numb with pity for Scarlet. No doubt she must have suffered this punishment often.

The only consolation was that I'd found another part of her diary, and successfully concealed it from Miss Fox. I'd had little time to worry about it during the caning. But now I was here with it in my hands, and I could read my sister's words, safe in the knowledge that everyone else would be downstairs in the dining hall. The diary entry shook in my hands, but I knew I had to be brave.

It began:

12th of September 1933

Dear Diary,

I have arrived at Rookwood! It's quite the adventure. I had to lug my suitcase up huge flights of stairs. They told me I'd be sharing a room with another girl, and that I was lucky because normally you have to start in one of the big dorms. I thought I wouldn't mind sharing though. I am a twin, after all.

But that was before I met her.

Her? Was this the same person Scarlet had been referring to before?

Violet Adams. I knew as soon as I saw her that she was going to be vile. Vile Violet! She took one look at my battered suitcase and glared at me like I was dirt on her shoe.

"Scholarship girl, are you?" she asked, and when I said yes she started trying to order me around. I told her I wasn't her maid, but she didn't seem to care. "If you can't afford to be here, then you should earn your keep," she said. Then she tossed her shoes at me.

I considered tossing them right back in her stuck-up face, but I knew Father would kill me if I got expelled on day one. So I just glowered at her and kept quiet.

I can't believe I have to share a room with that. I don't know how I'm going to stick it out until the end of term, let alone for a whole year.

Strange. I hadn't met anyone named Violet so far, hadn't even heard the name on the register. I flipped over to the next page.

Dear Diary,

Today was our first ballet class with the new school instructor. Her name is Miss Finch, and she dances beautifully. She told us that she had danced in theatres in Paris and Rome!

But then she hurt her leg badly and could no longer dance professionally. What a shame. If I were a world-famous dancer, I would insure my legs for thousands of pounds so that if I got injured I could retire to a life of luxury! I wouldn't want to be a teacher. Especially not in this awful place.

I felt a pang of sympathy for Miss Finch, losing everything she'd worked for... To dance in Paris or Rome was something I could only dream of, and it had been the same for Scarlet – though her dreams had always seemed more likely to come true somehow.

Miss Finch is so much better than Madame Everclear back home, that sour-faced old biddy! There's something about Miss Finch, when she dances. She looks so sad, like a china doll.

It's unfortunate that I have to share ballet class with Penny Winchester. She really is dreadful. She tried to trip me up every time I went past her for no reason at all. Later I saw her chatting to Violet. They were moaning about how they couldn't share a room, and when they caught me listening, they linked arms and stalked off. So I suppose that explains it.

Anyway, it's time for dinner now. If it's good, I shall try and sneak some extra helpings!

I chuckled a little at the last part, but underneath I felt a strong sense of unease. Penny was awful enough on her own, but this other girl sounded even worse. *Vile Violet* indeed.

I climbed out of bed to hide the pages away with the rest of the diary in the mattress, my sore limbs protesting all the while. Then I threw myself back on to my bed, grateful to lie still once more.

At about eight o'clock, just as my stomach was beginning to protest noisily, Ariadne ran into the room, her mousy hair bouncing with her.

"Scarlet!" she cried. "You weren't at dinner!"

I raised my eyebrows, which was about as much of a response as I could manage. Breathless, she looked down and noticed my cuts and bruises, not dissimilar to her own hockey-inflicted ones.

"Oh my goodness. What happened?"

I grimaced. "Miss Fox didn't approve of my trip to the stables."

Ariadne walked over to her bed and sat down on it heavily. "What? But... we're allowed to go there, aren't we?"

"I thought so. I..." I struggled for an explanation. "I just thought I'd have a look inside one of the stalls. And Miss Fox caught me. Apparently it belonged to her horse, and she thought I was going to play some sort of a prank on her."

Ariadne gasped. "Oh, how terrible!" I nodded slowly. Suddenly, she stood up and put her hands on her hips. "Well, you must rest!" she said.

I looked up at her in surprise. She pulled out my sheets and blankets from underneath me and tucked them up to my chin. "But..." I started.

"No buts!" Ariadne said. "Get some sleep and you will feel better."

She was right I hoped, and I *was* exhausted. I smiled at Ariadne gratefully.

So, sore as I was, I ended up having the best night's sleep I had ever had at Rookwood.

Chapter Twelve

The next morning, it took all of my effort to put on my uniform, comb my hair and drag myself to lessons. None of the teachers questioned my bruises – severe punishment was evidently not uncommon here, at least not with Miss Fox. Madame Lovelace did give me a sympathetic pat on the shoulder during history, but that just made me wince.

When evening came, I returned to the bathrooms, keen to soak my aching body. I went through the dimly lit corridor and into the damp room. I slid the bolt on the door and undressed as I ran the lukewarm water. It would have to do.

I stepped gingerly over the edge and lowered myself in. It wasn't the most pleasant bath I'd ever had, but not the coldest either (I thought of the swimming pool and shuddered).

As I lay there, I considered Scarlet's latest diary pages. I went through the words in my head, wondering if there was anything I'd missed.

But then I had a terrible realisation – the pages hidden in the stables were just old entries in her daily journal. They weren't something she'd ever intended as a message to me. There were no more clues.

And there might be no more letters to me from my sister, *ever*. I was on my own.

I sat up straight in the bathtub as tears streamed down my face and landed in the tepid water. It was bad enough losing my sister once, but now it seemed I had lost her in a different way. When I read what she'd written to me I heard her voice in my head like she was right beside me. It always sounded strong and happy, because that was Scarlet's way.

Even when she was spitting with anger, you could see this glimmer in her eye – the fiery passion she'd inherited from Father. Not that she'd ever admit it.

So here I was, alone in this god-forsaken place with nothing to guide me. Should I just give up? Grab all my things and run away…

Back to Aunt Phoebe?

Back home, to Father and my stepmother and horrid stepbrothers?

And what if I got caught? The last thing I wanted was to face punishment at the hands of Miss Fox again.

After I'd washed with Rookwood's pitiful regulation soap and heaved myself out of the bath, I looked at my blossoming bruises and was reminded of Ariadne's kindness. I couldn't just leave my only friend here either.

Someday soon, I was going to have to tell her the truth. Tell her that I wasn't really looking for a lost ring, that I wasn't even who she thought I was. Would she believe me? Would she refuse to speak to me ever again?

I didn't know, but there was one thing I felt sure of – if I couldn't trust Ariadne, I couldn't trust anyone.

When I woke up, light streaming in through the dorm window, Ariadne jumped out of her bed and excitedly informed me that it was Saturday.

"The weekend!" she shouted, far too cheerily for so early in the morning. "It's the second Saturday, in fact. That means we're allowed to leave the school grounds, right?"

I blinked. Perhaps this was one of the rules Miss Fox had told me in her office on the first day. "Oh yes," I said.

Ariadne was usually right about these things.

As we ate our meagre breakfast of lumpy porridge, Mrs Knight informed Ariadne that we were indeed allowed to walk to the local village of Rookwood. "There's not much there," she said. "A post office and a grocer's, and a church. That's about it."

I nodded along and attempted to look a bit bored, as if I was well familiar with the place. In truth, I was desperate to get out of the school. The past week had felt like a lifetime. It was like being trapped in an enormous box filled with people who hated me, or at least hated Scarlet. Even a trip to the post office – with nothing more to do than to watch people licking stamps – was preferable.

"Can I send a letter to my parents?" asked Ariadne.

"Of course," Mrs Knight replied. "But the postmaster puts aside any from pupils that don't have the official seal on them. The school has to check them first, you see."

Ariadne frowned. "Why?"

"I... I'm not totally sure. It's just the rules." Mrs Knight looked a little perturbed then, and Ariadne wisely stopped asking questions. I was pretty certain that I knew the reason – Miss Fox didn't want anyone bad-mouthing her precious school to their fee-paying parents. Thank goodness I hadn't tried to send that letter to Aunt Phoebe – who knows what trouble I'd have got into for that.

But maybe I could write to Aunt Phoebe again. I could be cryptic this time, write to her in riddles, like Scarlet would. And if it got through to her, she might be able to send help.

Back in our dorm, I waited impatiently for Ariadne to go to the lavatories and then retrieved the diary. As I took it out, I fumbled and some of the papers fell to the floor. I gathered them hurriedly, feeling like my secrets were spilling out for all to see. The words stared up at me: *Ivy, Penny, Violet, the Fox. You're the new me. Someone needs to know the truth.*

I flipped past a page with something scribbled about being hungry on it and the entry about Nadia, until I found my original letter to Aunt Phoebe. How things had changed in such a short time! I knew now that I had to be smarter, had to try to stay one step ahead of Miss Fox.

I carefully returned all the pages and hid the diary in my mattress once more. By the time Ariadne returned, I was sitting on my bed composing a new letter.

Dear Aunt Phoebe,

I hope you are well. Did you remember to water the plants? And have you got enough coal for the winter? Make sure you tell Mr Phillips from the village if you haven't got enough.

The school is certainly interesting. Remember when we got that letter, by the pond that day, what we talked about? I've found something relating to it. I hope I'll find out more soon.

Please write back.

  Best wishes,

  Your loving niece

There. I hope that would be vague enough to escape Miss Fox's attention. I almost signed my name, before realising I didn't know which to write. If I wrote 'Ivy' there was a chance that someone would see, and Miss Fox would be furious with me. And I couldn't write 'Scarlet', not unless I wanted to give my aunt a heart attack.

Once Ariadne had finished her own letter, we tucked them into envelopes in her satchel and got ready to leave.

"I'll go and get Miss Fox to seal them," she said. I smiled, grateful but wary. Would it pass scrutiny?

Thankfully Ariadne returned a short time later, looking only a little shaken. She was brandishing two freshly sealed letters, and soon we were walking down the great stone steps at the front of the school. The sun was bright, but in the shadow of the grand building the air was chilly.

"It's going to be wonderful," said Ariadne, tugging on my arm. "I'm going to buy apples and chocolate and..." She must have seen me wince, because she loosened her grip and took hold of my hand instead. "Sorry, do you feel a little better yet?"

"Oh, it's not too bad really," I said, trying to put on a

brave face. "Definitely improving. Thank you for getting the letters sealed. I'm not keen to see Miss Fox again in a hurry."

"Me neither. She's like the Wicked Witch of the West."

I laughed. "Maybe I should try throwing a bucket of water over her, and see if she melts!"

Ariadne giggled and then looked around guiltily, just in case Miss Fox happened to be following us out of the building.

"Be careful, Ariadne!" I said in a stage whisper. "She has spies everywhere!"

"Winged monkeys would be more like it!" she shrieked and ran ahead of me down the tree-lined drive. I chased after her, forgetting all about my aches and pains. Today I had a small taste of freedom.

The village was a short walk away, back through the dark archway of trees that lined the drive and down a twisting lane that led through fields of corn and barley. We followed the other girls but kept a safe distance as we joked about teachers and our fellow pupils.

We soon reached a white sign that read 'Rookwood' in black letters, the paint old and cracking. A little further on we came to the village green, a triangle of grass with a stone cross in the centre, a memorial to the Great War.

"The shop is near here," I said, looking around. I tried to

phrase it like a statement rather than a question.

"Over there?" said Ariadne.

Phew.

A group of schoolgirls were congregated in front of a building bearing the sign 'Kendall and Smith – Grocers'. Boxes of fruit and vegetables lined the street in front of the shop, under a striped awning.

I smiled. It was so wonderful just to be outside the school, and even though I had very little money to spare, the possibility of eating something that wasn't porridge or questionable meat was very exciting.

We ran over, only to realise that the girls standing in front of the shop were none other than Penny, Nadia and their faithful band of thieves: Clara Brand, Josephine Wilcox and Ethel Hadlow.

It was too late by the time I'd noticed. They had spotted us, and Penny was bearing down on me like a steam train.

She came over and shoved me, hard, and I fell back on to the grass.

"What was that for?" I asked, bewildered.

"You got Nadia a caning," Penny sneered, her copper hair glowing like embers in the sun. "That was payback!"

I stood up stiffly and smoothed out my dress. "But she was the one who pushed me into the swimming pool!"

Penny barely flinched at this news. "Well, I expect you

deserved it!" Ethel laughed, and it was not a friendly laugh.

Ariadne tugged on my arm. "Let's go back, Scarlet," she whispered, and I turned around, about to walk away. But the mention of my sister's name was like a slap to my memory.

Perhaps I didn't have to be Ivy right now. I could be *Scarlet*.

I turned back. Penny was mouthing something to her friends, who were all grinning like Cheshire cats. Before I knew what I was doing, I grabbed a handful of Penny's hair and tugged as hard as I could.

She shrieked and tried to bat me away, but I held my grip. "Just leave us alone, Penny!"

Nadia marched over. "You let go of her, Scarlet," she said.

"Gladly," I said, pulling a little harder. Penny hissed and tried her best to kick me in the shins. "As long as you go back to school and let us do what we want."

Nadia blinked her wide eyes at me. "Penny?" she said, uncertain.

"Yes, yes, all right!"

I let go of her hair, and several strands of it came off in my hands. She darted away from me, rubbing her scalp.

"Let's go," she said to her friends. Her face was flushed and her eyes were like thunder clouds. "I told you she was insane!"

The girls hurried away, leaving me standing breathless

in front of the shop. What had I done? I was frozen, heart pounding, strands of copper hair still clutched in my clammy hands.

I slowly turned around.

Ariadne was standing behind me on the green, her mouth hanging wide open.

"Ariadne?" She didn't move. I walked closer and waved my hand in front of her eyes. "A-Ariadne?"

"That. Was. Brilliant!" she said.

I breathed out. "Well, at least I got rid of them."

"I... you're so brave, Scarlet."

"That's one word for it." I winced. "Maybe 'insane' is another one."

Kendall and Smith's was bustling with activity. It seemed like half the village was in there, as well as a few groups of girls from school. It wasn't even a very big shop – it was about the size of one of our classrooms – with heavily stacked shelves lining the walls. Kendall (or possibly Smith) stood at the counter. He looked like he was about to do some hair pulling of his own.

Locals were shouting their weekly orders at him or grumbling amongst one another about the sudden invasion of schoolgirls. Some of the girls were waving purchases in his direction. "One at a time!" he shouted. "Please form an orderly queue!"

Ariadne went straight for the jars of sweets, and I followed her. The candies in each jar sparkled with the sugar coating and my mouth watered.

"How much money do you have?" I asked Ariadne. In response she pulled out a green purse from her satchel that jangled as she moved it.

"A lot." She grinned. "My daddy sends me an allowance."

"Lucky you! I don't think my Father is even speaking to me. Come to think of it, I'm not really speaking to him either."

"Why?" asked Ariadne, suddenly looking sad.

Oops. What could I say? He sent me to this awful school, where my sister died, without even a word... and I'm currently impersonating her?

I curled my hand into a fist. "No reason," I said. "We just don't get on."

"Oh," said Ariadne. "Well, never mind. I'll share my money with you! Now we can finally have that midnight feast."

"Brilliant!" I replied.

On the way out of the shop, I felt a tap on my shoulder. I thought at first that it was Nadia, come back to get revenge for what I did for Penny. But this girl was taller, and older.

"I'm sorry about my sister," she said in a soft accent, as we stepped out into the street. I must have looked bewildered, because she continued, "I saw what happened earlier. Nadia should not be friends with that girl. She's trouble."

I nodded. "You can say that again."

Nadia's sister smiled. "My name is Meena. What's yours?"

"I— Scarlet."

"Scarlet," she repeated. She held out her hand, and I shook it gingerly. "I will try to get her to leave you alone. But I cannot promise anything. She longs to fit in, and since what happened with that girl Violet, Penny had an opening for a best friend. I hope you understand."

"Meena!" called some older girls from the other side of the green, waving at her. She hurried away after them, smiling back at me as she went.

I wanted to call after her, to ask her what she meant about Violet, but I realised how foolish that would be. *Scarlet* would already know.

Meanwhile Ariadne had picked up a peculiar fruit from the stand and was scrutinising it intently. Once I'd grabbed her, we stopped off at the post office to send our letters, with Ariadne insisting on using her money to pay for both of our stamps. I prayed that Aunt Phoebe might sense that something was wrong from my strange letter, that she'd see it was a cry for help. That Miss Fox wouldn't intercept it and throw it away. But I felt that my chances were slim.

116

*

That night, we shut the door to our room and wedged some dirty linen under it to make sure no light or sound got out. I didn't know the punishment for eating sweets in the middle of the night, and I didn't want to find out.

Ariadne lit a candle and we laid out our provisions in the semi-darkness. We had pear drops, aniseed balls, liquorice, sugared almonds, mint humbugs and chocolate fudge. It was the best picnic I'd ever seen.

"You'll have to thank your father, Ariadne," I said.

She sighed. "I will. I just wish I could see him. Letters and money aren't the same, you know?"

"I know. But let's not be sad," I replied, sounding more cheerful than I really felt. "We have the finest midnight feast in history!"

Ariadne smiled in the flickering candlelight. "But now we have a difficult decision to make... What do we eat first?"

An hour later, we had eaten more sweets than a person should probably consume in a lifetime. I lay back against my bed frame, blissfully content. Ariadne was telling me about how she had a whole wardrobe full of dresses at home and was describing each one in painstaking detail.

"And I have this beautiful jewellery box too – it's full of necklaces and bracelets and rings and... Oh, Scarlet,

I'm sorry! I forgot about your ring…"

I blinked. I think I had been seconds away from sleep. "What?"

"Your gold ring! I'm so sorry. You must think me such a show-off, when you've lost your treasured possession." She whacked herself in the head with a feather pillow, and I tried my best not to laugh.

"It's fine," I said.

"Have you tried looking under your bed?" she asked, suddenly. "Sometimes when I lose things, that's where they turn up. I always think there's a little goblin who likes to steal things and hide them under beds."

"Oh…" I started, my tired mind struggling to form a sentence. *Of course I've looked there*, I was going to say. *First place I tried. No need to investigate.*

But I didn't say it quick enough, and Ariadne was already on her hands and knees on the carpet, the candleholder in her hands.

"I think the stuffing is leaking out of your mattress," she said.

Oh no…

I leapt in front of Ariadne. "I've looked there already!" I said, sounding a lot more panicked than necessary. But she just peered around me into the dark. "No no, it's fine!"

I put my hand in my mouth and bit it, trying not to say

anything. If she discovered the diary...

But a few moments later, Ariadne came out backwards, the little stub of her candle glowing brightly. "There's a hole in your mattress," she said plainly. "No sign of your ring, though."

I held my breath, waiting for the inevitable questions, but they didn't come. She just sat down, picked up the last mint humbug and sucked it thoughtfully.

"Well, it is quite uncomfortable," was all I could think to say.

Ariadne nodded, then yawned widely. "What time is it?"

I glanced out at the night sky through our thin curtains. "I've no idea," I said. "Maybe around one in the morning."

"Well, I think I shall go to bed. Goodnight, Scarlet."

"Goodnight, Ariadne."

We both got into our beds. As quietly as I could, I let out a sigh of relief. The diary was safe for another day.

But how much longer could I keep it a secret?

Chapter Thirteen

That Sunday, it rained. It tapped relentlessly on the stained-glass windows of the school chapel. It drummed on the roof and spilled from the gutters, and the caretaker was forced to put out buckets to collect the drips. But most of all, it prevented us from going outside.

We lay in our room all day. I read while Ariadne practised her sewing, which she already seemed to excel at and therefore didn't need to practise. The matron came to change our sheets and do laundry, and at six o'clock we went down for dinner – what I assumed was an attempt at roast beef – where I saw Miss Fox again for the first time since the caning.

She was back in her place at one end of the dining room, her faithful cane by her side. Her expression was as acidic as usual. I nervously avoided her gaze.

I'd just disposed of my cutlery in the bowl for cleaning when the Fox appeared right behind me. I almost smashed my plate in shock.

"I do hope you'll be on your best behaviour for lessons tomorrow, Scarlet Grey," she said sharply.

"Of course, M-Miss," I stuttered, edging away from her.

She stepped sideways. "I mean it. I don't want to have to see you in my office again."

"I understand." I couldn't bear another beating, nor did I have any wish to stare into the eyes of those eerie stuffed dogs for a minute longer than necessary.

"I sincerely hope so. I'll be keeping an eye on you."

Had she ever not been keeping an eye on me? I shuddered at the thought, and hurried out of the dining room.

I had butterflies, moths and possibly a whole host of other insects in my stomach as I prepared for ballet the next day. I was scared I'd get everything wrong, especially since I was still rather sore. I felt calmer when I finally entered the studio.

At least it wasn't a swimming lesson.

I headed to the *barre* and began my warm-up. Although my muscles were less stiff, the stretches weren't exactly comfortable. As I practised, I observed the rest of the class in the mirror. Nadia had chosen a spot as far away from me as possible. She looked my way at one point and glared, so I grimaced back at her, making her start in shock. I caught sight of my expression in the mirror – truly terrifying in the orange gaslight – and had to resist the urge to laugh. I resumed my straight face and carried on.

When we moved to centre work, I began to feel like I was getting back on form. "Your *grand battement* is well controlled," said Miss Finch, pleasantly. She turned. "Nadia, that is not fifth position. I'm not even sure that's any position!"

I risked a smile of my own at that.

To my relief, Nadia continued to leave me well alone. Perhaps I had scared her off? I hoped that the same would be true for Penny.

It was only as the class concluded and I went to unlace my shoes that I had a thought – unlike the dining hall, the ballet studio was a place that was often deserted, as well as being a place that was important to Scarlet. Miss Finch couldn't be there *all* the time. If I returned at night, I could search the place uninhibited...

"Scarlet?" called Miss Finch's voice.

I looked up. "Yes, Miss?"

"Class is over," she said. "You can go now."

I looked around – I'd just been sitting on the floor, my shoes half unlaced. "Oh yes. Sorry." I hurried to take them off and put my regular shoes back on.

It seemed like my life nowadays was just one big apology.

When night came, I waited for Ariadne to fall asleep. This didn't take long, since she was thoroughly exhausted from playing hockey. She started snoring, but I decided to wait a while longer to make sure everyone else was asleep too. I hoped that all the adults still in the school, like the matron, would go to bed fairly early.

After what felt like ages, I changed out of my nightgown and into my black leotard and skirt. Hopefully they would help me blend into the shadows. Once again I went barefoot. I didn't want to damage my ballet shoes, and anything else would be too loud.

I took a deep breath and opened the door slowly. When I was sure that the coast was clear, I darted out as nimbly as I could in the direction of the staircase.

It was pitch black, so I had to feel for the walls. Eventually I reached a gap that I knew to be the stairs and made my way down.

The school was silent. My light steps seemed louder than hammers as they echoed on the wooden stairs. I kept close to the edge, hoping I could hide quickly if anyone came along.

At the bottom of the stairs was the corridor that led past several of the classrooms, and eventually to the door to the basement containing the studio. My heart was thumping in my chest. I didn't even dare to imagine what the punishment would be if I were caught.

I peered in each direction, but it was useless in the dark. I could barely see my own hands. *At least*, I thought, *that means no one can see me either. Hopefully.*

I felt my way along, until my hand hit metal hinges. Standing back, I could just about make out the familiar door. I pushed the handle down gently, and the door swung inwards, making only the faintest of creaking noises. I still checked over my shoulder, though. Just in case.

When I looked back down, I noticed a warm orange glow from the bottom of the stairs. A few steps inside, I could smell the gas lamps. Strange for them to still be burning at this time of night.

I froze and fought the urge to run. What if someone was down there? I stood flat against the cold stone wall and listened. If there was a person in the studio, they were alone.

I pulled the door shut behind me and made a tentative step downwards. What was the worst that could happen?

Well, the absolutely worst would be Miss Fox, of course. But that was unlikely. The ballet room was Miss Finch's domain. Even though she was a teacher, I didn't think she would do anything more than chastise me.

It was now or never.

I went slowly, like walking through water. When I finally reached the studio I was surprised to find it completely empty.

I waited a few seconds. I was almost convinced it was a trap, that a page of Scarlet's diary would be on a golden plinth at the end of the room, and that when I touched it Miss Fox would leap out and shout, "Aha!"

I walked out into the centre of the floor. The cold chilled me to the bone, and the wooden floorboards felt rough on my bare feet. The flickering of the gas lamps distorted everything, bending the shadows. I headed for the piano at the far end, large and black, almost like a shadow itself.

And then I caught sight of my reflection.

It was *Scarlet*.

I don't know what it was: the darkness or the strange light or the cold air. But for some reason, I wasn't *just* seeing me, the twin who looked like Scarlet. I was seeing *her* there, trapped behind the glass, her big eyes looking out at me. Pleading.

I took a few steps forward. So did the girl in the mirror. As I got closer, I reached out my hand, and touched my fingers to the icy surface. Instantly, I was back in our childhood home, Scarlet copying my movements on the other side of the window.

"Scarlet," I whispered, a tear rolling down my cheek.

I moved a little, and saw the image reflected a thousand times. I spun around, and I saw a thousand Scarlets.

I was not alone.

And I began to dance.

I danced, and I watched as the reflection, Scarlet, danced alongside me. She flipped her head as I did, she leapt into a *grand jeté* when I did. Her footsteps followed mine across the floor. In my head I could almost hear the extra set of echoes from her feet.

No matter what I did, she was there. She was everywhere, and the reflections spun around me until I began to feel dizzy and shut my eyes. But there she was, in my head, dancing with me for one final time, my twin.

As I went into a *fouetté en tournant*, I lost my balance and I stumbled...

And fell straight at the feet of Miss Finch.

"You didn't turn your head," she said.

Chapter Fourteen

I blinked up at her. For a moment I stopped still as my brain whirred and then I scrambled to my feet.

"What are you doing down here?" she asked.

"I-I wanted to practise," I said. Miss Finch's eyes widened but I continued. "I haven't danced in ages, and... I felt like I was getting behind the others."

I was vaguely aware of the reflections all around us, the illusion of Scarlet had faded. There was only me and Miss Finch now.

"Well, that's diligent of you," she said, "but you do

realise it's the middle of the night?"

I nodded. And I was about to say that I couldn't sleep, that I was terribly sorry and wouldn't do it again. But instead another question came to mind. "Why are you still here, Miss?"

She looked taken aback, but after a moment she walked over to the piano seat and sat down with a sigh. "It's complicated."

"You could explain it to me. I'm pretty good at listening."

Her eyes flicked up, the light of the gas lamps dancing across them. "Not at listening to the rules, apparently."

I blushed.

"The place I have to sleep is not ideal," she said, staring up at the arches in the stone ceiling. "But down here it's quiet, and I can be alone to think about things. The cold is a problem, though."

"Oh yes," I said, readily agreeing with her.

Miss Finch wrapped her knitted cardigan tighter around herself. "Can I ask you something, Scarlet?" she said.

I had to admit, I flinched a little. Something in the way she said the name made it sound so wrong. "Of course."

"Why do you want to be a dancer?"

I turned her question over in my mind. "Because it's beautiful. It's an art, isn't it?"

She frowned a little. "You don't want to be in the

spotlight? To be a *prima ballerina*, touring the world? To be showered with flowers and gifts every night?"

That seemed like something Scarlet would want. Had Miss Finch asked her the same question?

As I looked at Miss Finch, her small body seeming frail with her knees tucked up on the piano stool, it wasn't Scarlet's answer I wanted to give.

"No," I replied. "I just want to be able to dance. Those other things... they don't matter. Not to me, anyway."

"You would turn it down?" she asked, raising an eyebrow.

"Oh, of course not. But the dancing is enough for me."

"Hmm."

This was some sort of test, and she was deciding whether or not I had passed. But before I could consider this, she stood up.

"You're right," she said. "Of course you're right." She tucked a lock of her auburn hair behind her ear. "Goodness, it's so late. You really should be in bed. *I* should be in bed."

I nodded. But I hadn't searched the studio! What if Miss Finch was down here every night, and I never had the chance again?

"Go on, then," she said, gesturing towards the stairs.

I hesitated. "But... if Miss Fox..."

"She usually goes to bed at ten o'clock sharp. Couldn't have her finding out about me staying down here after hours, could I?" Miss Finch smiled mischievously. It was an odd expression to see on the face of a teacher.

"So there's no chance of me being caught?"

"I can't say that," she waved a hand dismissively, "but if you run into the matron, perhaps tell her you're feeling unwell."

"All right," I said. There didn't seem to be anything I could do. "Well, thank you for not giving me the cane."

She gave me a look like I'd just told her I was a cabbage. "Why would I do that?"

"Because I'm breaking multiple rules?"

Her expression didn't change. "Oh," she said.

I was beginning to wonder if Miss Finch wasn't all there.

"I shall go then," I said. "Goodnight, Miss."

"Goodnight," she replied.

I walked out of the amber glow and into the darkness of the stairwell. I took a backward glance over my shoulder, and saw that Miss Finch was staring at her own reflection.

I'd got off lightly, but now I had a bigger problem – the ballet studio had become out of bounds.

Just as Miss Finch had said, there was no sign of any prowling teachers upstairs. I made it back to my bed without meeting a soul, and I was so tired that sleep came easily. But when my eyes flicked open the next day, with the light of dawn spilling in the window, my first thought was of Scarlet's diary.

Unless I found a day when Miss Finch wasn't present, I wouldn't be able to search the studio *ever*.

I rolled over with a sigh. My bed sheets were surprisingly warm, and I fought the urge to slip back into sleep.

Ariadne woke up soon after I did, rubbing her eyes as she sat up. "Mmmfmorning," she said.

"Mmmfmorning indeed," I replied, pulling myself upright.

"I wonder what's for breakfast today? I'm *so* hungry."

Unsurprisingly, it was porridge. I'd managed to convince the cook to give me an extra spoonful of honey, though, so it wasn't too terrible. I sat down at my usual place. Ariadne was looking despondently into her bowl.

"You didn't get any honey?" I asked.

"No," she said. "I asked, but she just gave me a look and said, 'Next'."

"Hmm. I suppose someone was smiling in my favour today. Here, have mine. We'll swap."

"Really?" she said, her face lighting up as I handed her my bowl of sweet porridge. "Oh, thank you, Scarlet. You're the best!"

"That's kind of you," said Mrs Knight from across the table, watching Ariadne shovel down her considerably improved breakfast. Then, "Slow down a little, Miss Flitworth, you can't be *that* hungry."

There it was, that word again. It echoed in my head as I stared at my tiny Scarlet-like reflection upside down in my spoon.

And then I realised why.

Hungry.

That scribble I'd seen on the back of one of the diary pages, something about being hungry. Now I thought about it, how could it not be a clue? Scarlet never wrote on the back of her pages, she said it made the ink smudgy!

When you're hungry... you go to the dining hall.

I slammed the spoon into the table so hard I made myself jump. Ariadne squeaked. I looked around – we were surrounded by chatting girls, teachers and dinner ladies.

There was nothing else for it – I would have to make another night-time expedition. At least I now knew that Miss Fox was unlikely to be around.

Or, at least, that's what I hoped.

By the end of the day, after another excruciating assembly, I was itching to begin my search. I waited for Ariadne to bury her head under the pillow, and then pulled on a woollen jumper over my nightgown. I sneaked through the dark corridors and down the stairs once more, but this time went in the opposite direction to the ballet studio.

I wondered if Miss Finch was down there still. What did

she do? Sit and read? Perhaps she stood alone, under the gas lamps, trying to dance on her crippled leg. The thought made me feel rather sad.

The wide wooden doors of the dining hall were shut but, thankfully, not locked. I pushed one open and it swung too far and banged against the wall. I glanced around anxiously in case someone had heard.

The hall had high windows, and the glow of the moon spilled in. Everything was bathed in silvery-grey light – the rows of long wooden tables, the metal-legged chairs. The silence was heavy around me.

I walked the perimeter of the room, feeling the rough wall paint as I went, looking for hiding places. But there were no mouse holes, no loose bits of floorboard.

Then I started looking under the tables. I tried to picture Scarlet getting on her hands and knees with a roll of packing tape to secure her diary pages underneath. Even in my imagination, it seemed unlikely.

But after I'd searched under a third table, getting my nightgown thoroughly dusty, I realised the scope of my task. There were so many tables – and chairs too! – that there was no way of knowing which to check. Surely Scarlet didn't expect me to look under every single one? I was beginning to feel like this might just be madness.

And besides, what if someone brushed their leg up against

it, or a maid found it? They often put the chairs upside down on top of the tables in order to clean the floor.

I looked around the vast, deserted hall. What else was in here?

The serving hatch in the far wall drew my eye. It was shut, but there was a red door next to it that led into the kitchen, where dinner ladies usually bustled in and out, their arms laden with plates.

Well, it had to be worth a try. I went over and tentatively tried the door handle. *Drat! Locked.*

Flustered by my failure, I gave the kitchen door a kick, bruising my toe in the process. I sank down against the cold wall. What an idiot I was! Did I expect every door to be open?

And as I sat there, my head in my hands, wondering what to do next, I heard a little voice say, "Scarlet?"

I jumped up instantly, preparing my excuses. *I was sleepwalking, I was hungry, I was lost, I was...*

But the voice wasn't that of a teacher. It had sounded like...

"Scarlet?" As I looked over to the doors, I saw a familiar mousy face peering back at me.

Ariadne.

Chapter Fifteen

Ariadne stood there, clad only in her long cotton nightgown. I climbed up from the floor. "What's the matter?" she whispered. "What are you doing down here?"

"What are *you* doing down here?" I hissed, and immediately felt terrible as her face fell.

"I couldn't sleep," she said dejectedly. "I was worrying about hockey. And then I saw you get out of bed, so I-I followed you."

"You followed me? I might have been going to the

lavatories or something!"

"Yes, but..." She looked ashamed. "The other night I could've sworn I saw you putting on your ballet outfit." Suddenly her eyes filled with light. "And besides, you didn't go to the lavatories, did you? You came down here and searched the entire dining hall. And now you're getting angry with the kitchen door! What's going on, Scarlet?"

I put my face in my hands. I had definitely underestimated Ariadne's curiosity. And what's more, I had run out of excuses.

"Well?" said Ariadne. "You can tell me. I'm your friend, aren't I?"

"Of course," I replied. At least, I hoped so. I wasn't sure she would be after this. Could I trust her?

I walked over and sat down on a chair in the moonlight. "You might want to sit down for this."

Ariadne followed me and pulled up a chair. "All right."

I took a deep breath. "I'm not Scarlet," I said.

"What?" Her face contorted in confusion. This wasn't going to be easy. I stared up at the light fixtures dangling from the ceiling, hoping for some inspiration.

"I'm not Scarlet. The truth is... Scarlet is... *was* my twin sister. My name is Ivy."

"Wait, what? What happened to Scarlet? And why are you pretending to be her?"

"Scarlet's gone. She died, here at Rookwood, last year. And Miss Fox forced me to impersonate her from the beginning of term. I don't know why, but..."

Suddenly the enormity of everything rushed in and threatened to drown me. What was I going along with? I'd always believed what I'd been told with all my heart, that Scarlet had died of a sudden flu and there was nothing they could have done. I'd clung to that. But everything about this felt wrong. What if something far, *far* more sinister was going on?

My voice cracked up. "I think something bad – really bad – went on here. But I have no idea what."

Ariadne's face crumpled. "The real Scarlet is dead? Oh gosh, I'm so sorry... I can't..."

My stomach lurched, but I managed a nod.

"And they're making you pretend to be her? That's just wrong, that's—"

"Yes." I winced. "I had no choice. And now I'm caught up in it all and I need to know the truth." A thought occurred, so horrible it took all my strength not to force it back down. "What if... what if she was murdered, Ariadne? *My twin!*"

Ariadne fell silent, her eyes wide and frightened. After some time she said, "I'm so sorry... this is awful. But why are you trying to get into the kitchen in the middle of the night?"

I blinked back my tears and the truth finally spilled out.

"Well, you see, I need to find her diary. She left pieces of it for me all over the school, with clues. At least... some of them were definitely clues. I'm not so sure about this one. It just said something about being hungry."

"You didn't really lose your ring," said Ariadne, shrewdly.

"No. I'm sorry I lied to you, Ariadne. I'm the worst friend ever." I hung my head.

"Are you kidding?"

"What?" I looked up.

"*This so exciting!*" Ariadne jumped to her feet, her expression suddenly alive. "A real mystery! I'll help you, Scarlet. Ivy, I mean. We'll do it together!"

I was astonished. "Aren't you angry with me? I deceived you... I'm deceiving everyone."

"Never mind that. You've told me the truth now, and no one *ever* tells me the truth." She pulled me up from the chair. "I didn't know Scarlet, so as far as I'm concerned you're still the same person, just with a different name. We'll find out what happened to your sister. I promise!"

"Thank you," I whispered. "All right. Let's do it. But we need to take things one step at a time. How are we going to get through the kitchen door?"

Ariadne walked over and tried the handle. It was no good, of course. But then she got down on her knees and peered into the lock. "I can pick this," she said.

"Excuse me?" Now it was my turn to be bewildered.

She pulled a couple of bobby pins out of her hair and made a few attempts at twisting them around the inside. There was a *click*.

Ariadne stood up and opened the door, leaving me gaping at her.

As she slid the bobby pins back into her hair, Ariadne shrugged. "My governess used to shut me in the airing cupboard when I wouldn't do my sums. But I was resourceful!"

The kitchen windows were small and it was quite a bit darker than in the dining hall, but there was a pile of white candles and a small book of matches on a shelf by the door. I lit one, and as it flickered into life I got my first glimpse of the Rookwood kitchen.

There was a large black iron range surrounded by plenty of worktops and drawers, a brand-new refrigerator and a deep ceramic sink. A vast wooden table took up the space in the centre of the room. The ceiling was hung with meat hooks, not currently holding any meat, thank goodness.

There was also a dumb waiter in one corner, a big imposing wooden cabinet built into the wall with a winch to send it up and down. I'd seen one before in Bramley Hollow Manor, back in my aunt's village.

"Where should we look first?" whispered Ariadne. She had lit a candle of her own and held it out in front of her, her face glowing in the darkness.

"I'm not sure," I replied. "Maybe the drawers?"

It turned out that opening drawers quietly is extremely difficult, especially when they're full of cutlery and utensils. Ariadne and I went around the entire room, pulling out each one as carefully as we could.

"Don't forget the tops of them," I said, sticking my arm in at an awkward angle as I tried to feel the top of the drawer.

"Ouch!"

"What?"

"Knife."

"Oh."

The search was proving fruitless. In fact, it was a pretty fruitless kitchen in general. The only plant product I'd seen so far was a wilting cabbage.

"Cupboards?" asked Ariadne. I nodded in agreement and got down on my knees.

The first one I opened was full of plates of varying sizes. I held my candle as close as I could, trying to get a good look at the inside. There was nothing obvious, so I began feeling around the edges to make sure.

Ariadne was doing the same in the cupboard to my left, which was full of jars. Her look of excitement seemed to be fading into one of worry. She turned to me.

"What happens if we get caught, Scar— Ivy? What will Miss Fox do to us?"

"Give us a caning for stealing, I imagine." I trembled at the thought.

"But we're not stealing. We're looking for diary pages."

"We're not going to tell Miss Fox that, though, are we! If she catches us, we'll... we'll tell her we were taking food. For a midnight feast. She might just believe it."

"All right," said Ariadne, her face still grave. "I don't want to be caned," she added, in a mousy squeak.

I stood up. "I'll tell her it was me, that I coerced you into doing it. That she'll *definitely* believe."

Ariadne nodded and then peered in amongst the jars. "Ooh! I think I've found something."

"What is it?" I hissed, jumping down beside her. I held my candle out, trying to see what she'd got. "Paper?"

"Yes! But... oh no..." She pulled her hand out of the cupboard. It had a square of white stuck to it. "Fly paper." She grimaced.

I didn't know whether to laugh or cry. "Drat," I said, hitting my hand on the wooden door in frustration.

Ariadne flapped her hand in the air, attempting to detach herself from the fly paper. It had a couple of unfortunate flies stuck to it too. "Yuck."

We were running out of places to search, and I could feel my desperation piling up. I rifled through the rest of the cupboards. They were full of the usual kitchen things, foodstuffs, scales, rolling pins, baking dishes. It seemed quite a variety for a place that seemed to produce only stews and porridge.

Ariadne was still trying to peel the fly paper off. She hadn't even put down her candle. "Look," I said, speaking from experience, thanks to pranks pulled by my nasty stepbrothers. "You need to stick it to something else, or it'll never come off. Try the table. And then you'll have to wash your hands. It's got arsenic in it, I think."

Ariadne looked horrified and rushed to the table immediately, making disgusted noises. I took hold of her candle and stubbed it out. She put her hand down on the table and the paper stuck to it firmly. "Phew," she said.

That was somewhere we hadn't yet looked, I realised – the big table. So I got down on my hands and knees once again. The kitchen floor was no cleaner than the one in the dining hall.

"What are you doing?" whispered Ariadne.

"Checking under here," I breathed. The table was so vast and tall that I could comfortably lift my head up underneath it. I looked at the tarnished dark wood by the light of my candle, searching it for a familiar white rectangle. And then I saw it.

"Please, let this not be fly paper," I muttered, crawling towards it.

"Did you find anything?" asked Ariadne, her upside-down head appearing at the side of the table. "It's dark up here," she said uncertainly.

I peeled off the paper and unfolded it.

It was Scarlet's handwriting! Just two words and an arrow:

Look down

↓

I scrambled back out from under the table to where Ariadne was waiting, and relit her candle with my own. "I found this," I told her, holding out the paper.

She scrutinised it. "Look down? Look down where?"

We both stared at the floor as if it would reveal something. But there wasn't anything there, nor was there anything else we could look under.

"Hmm," Ariadne said, and I could almost see the thoughts moving across her face in the candlelight.

"It must be out of sight, of course. And... somewhere down... Aha!" She clicked her fingers and then grinned at me expectantly.

"What?"

"We don't have to just *look down*, we have to look, down." She pointed. "Downstairs! Below this room. That must be what Scarlet meant."

"But I don't even know *how* to get downstairs. Or what's down there."

But Ariadne was looking behind me, and I followed her gaze. *The dumb waiter*.

"No. Oh no." It was one thing to search the kitchens at night, and quite another to ride the dumb waiter into a deep, dark cellar. "You really think so?"

I went over to the dumb waiter and unlatched the wooden door. I could make out the wooden box and the ropes it was suspended from. I leant inside and put my weight on it, and it seemed to hold – and there was something grainy in the bottom. Flour, I guessed.

"I think they haul up sacks of flour in this thing," I whispered to Ariadne. "It should be able to take my weight." *Should*, I thought.

Ariadne gulped. "I'll lower you down..."

And that was how I ended up contorting myself into a dumb waiter in the middle of the night. It was incredibly cramped and the flour tickled my nose, threatening to make me sneeze. My elbows and knees bumped on the sides, and I realised I was probably giving myself bruises on top of bruises.

"Ready?" asked Ariadne.

"Do it," I said.

She began winching the dumb waiter down. I could hear the quiet whirring of the ropes as they went around the pulley. Darkness slipped before my eyes as I descended through the floor.

Eventually the contraption pulled to a halt, and I unfolded myself into the cold cellar. It was a cavernous place and the shadows crept towards me. I held out my candle, my hand shaking. The stone floor was covered with bags of flour, along with other supplies – tinned meats and soups, boxes of crackers, sacks of potatoes and porridge oats.

But that wasn't all. As I held up my candle, I saw rows and rows of bottles glinting darkly at me. Great wine racks covered the walls as far as I could see. No doubt a treat for the teachers. Or perhaps it was Mr Bartholomew's personal collection?

I tiptoed past the piles of provisions and stopped in front of the nearest rack. The first thing I noticed was that under each bottle was a different number – no, a year.

Scarlet would have picked something significant, I was sure of it. I tried the year we were born, 1922, but the bottle was full of wine and there was nothing behind it.

Something else, then, maybe another important date? Perhaps something to do with the diary... Aha! What about the year that Scarlet had come to Rookwood, 1933?

I followed the rack along to the end, but to my disappointment there was no bottle for 1933. It must have been too recent. So I had to go for something a bit further back. Father's birthday was a possibility – but no, there was no love lost between him and Scarlet. But then there was our mother. If I remembered rightly, she had been born in 1899.

I dashed down the years, hoping that my hunch was right. And there, dusty but still present, was the bottle labelled 1899. I pulled it out and – yes! I couldn't believe my luck. It had been emptied of wine and there were pages rolled up inside – a whole wad of them. "A fine vintage," I whispered.

Remembering Ariadne was alone upstairs, I hurried back to the dumb waiter, still clutching the wine bottle. I climbed into the box and knocked on the top of it.

For a moment nothing happened, but then the whole thing lurched and I almost dropped the bottle. I clasped it to my chest as the dumb waiter creaked up the shaft.

At the top, I was greeted with Ariadne's worried face. "Did you find anything?" she asked.

I untangled my limbs and then nodded, breathless,

holding out the bottle to her.

She gasped audibly. "A message in a bottle! How thrilling!"

I pulled out the cork with a *pop* and tipped the papers out, then hid the empty bottle at the back of a cupboard. "We've got to get out of here," I whispered.

We blew out the candles and returned them to the pile. With any luck, nobody would notice they'd been used. But as we hurried out into the dining hall, I heard something rustle behind us. Swiftly followed by a loud *crash*.

Ariadne and I looked at each other.

"Run!" I yelled.

Chapter Sixteen

We ran through the pitch darkness and up the stairs as fast as our legs would carry us. Neither of us wanted a taste of the cane.

I was still clutching the diary pages tightly in my hand as we reached the door of room thirteen. I flung it open, forgetting to worry about the noise. Ariadne pulled it shut behind us and we both dived into our beds.

I tugged the blankets right up over my head. We were both silent, not even daring to breathe.

Slowly, I began to realise that no one had followed us.

We'd got away with it. A laugh bubbled up in my throat. Ariadne joined in, and I had to bury my face in the pillow to keep from becoming hysterical.

"That was *brilliant*! We did it!" she whispered.

I pulled my face from the pillow. "Yes, we did," I said quietly. Then I unfolded the pages on to my blanket and began to read aloud in a whisper:

Dear Diary,

I think Violet has been going through my things. When I got back to the dorm after lessons, everything had been moved. Only slightly, but enough for me to notice the difference. I yelled at her, but she just acted all innocent. She thinks everything in our room belongs to her. I caught her using my curling pins just the other day. It's bad enough that she steals my ink and paper whenever I'm not looking.

"Who's Violet?" asked Ariadne.

"I don't know," I replied. "I've only heard about her from the diary."

Clearly, she is quite the spoiled brat. I told her I thought as much. "You don't know a thing about me," was her response. Actually, I do know a fair bit. I know that her father was this shipping magnate named Harold Adams, who was filthy rich. And

I'd also heard that her parents had been attending a grand ball on one of his ships when it was sunk off the coast of America, and that she'd been orphaned. They left her an enormous pile of money, and she's never wanted for anything. I can believe it. She has all these fine clothes and jewels — why anyone would bring them to this school, I can't imagine.

"Scarlet was jealous, I'll bet," I explained. "She'd wear fancy clothes and jewels anywhere if she got the chance."

She expects me to do things for her, but I won't. I just won't! And then she gets cross with me, finds anything she can pick on me about. "Scarlet, have you put on weight?" "Scarlet, don't you think you should brush your hair?" "Scarlet, how did you pass the entrance exam, exactly?"

Some days she doesn't bother me. She doesn't speak a word, just sits on her side of the room in a brooding silence. But that almost worries me more. I wouldn't put it past her to smother me in my sleep.

I miss Ivy.

Underlined twice? I was surprised, somehow. Even though we were twins, I'd always felt that it was me who clung to Scarlet. It had never occurred to me that she might need me too.

I heard a sniffle from Ariadne.

That wasn't the only thing that had jumped out at me... Surely Scarlet must have been joking. She was always so dramatic – I felt certain that Violet was just a schoolgirl, another bully, nothing worse.

Feeling wary, I unfolded the remaining pages.

Dear Diary,

Violet was insufferable today. You won't believe what she did. I was working on an assignment at my desk, and she put a cup of boiling water down on the flat of my hand. I managed to knock it on to the floor, but my hand was scalded. She just walked off, laughing.

I curled my own hand in anger. What an awful girl. *Poor Scarlet.*

The nurse made me rinse it with the cold tap, but I could tell she didn't believe me when I said that Violet had done it. The brat is such a goody-goody in front of the teachers. They all feel sorry for her, I think. They don't know her like I do. And besides, why don't they feel sorry for ME? I've lost people too.

I had to get away from her somehow – so I wandered around the school, and you know what I found? There's this hatch that goes out on to the rooftops. There's steps up to it and you can push it open and climb out. Whoever last used it must have forgotten to lock it.

I climbed up, of course. Who wouldn't? There's a flat bit of roof with tiles sloping around it. I nestled in amongst the chimney stacks and watched the sky. Swallows dived around my head and clouds drifted slowly past. It was beautiful and cold and, most importantly, there was not a soul around but me. I stayed there until the sun dipped below the horizon and I started to shiver so much that I had to go back inside.

It's my secret place now. Violet was already in bed when I got back, fast asleep. At last I have something that she hasn't. She can't take this away from me.

I smiled weakly. At least Scarlet had found some sanctuary at Rookwood. "I wonder if we can get up there? On the roof?" I asked Ariadne.

She yawned. "Mmmaybe."

Holding my breath, I turned the page over and, sure enough, there was something else written there.

It said simply, Look for number one.

"It says 'Look for number one'."

"Hmm, numbers," she mumbled. "Or a metaphor... or something."

I was delighted to have the next clue, but my eyelids suddenly felt unbearably heavy and I couldn't help yawning.

"Let's investigate some more tomorrow. And... Ariadne?"

"Mmm?"

"Thank you. For still being my friend."

I couldn't see her smile in the darkness, but I could almost feel it beaming off her. And it wasn't long before we were both fast asleep.

I woke up in a panic. Where were the diary pages?

I leapt out of bed and frantically searched the sheets, only to find them crumpled up in one corner. I clutched them to my chest with relief. I really had to be more careful.

Ariadne was staring at me from her bed. "Do you always hide those?" she asked.

"Oh yes," I said earnestly. "Don't forget, no one can know about this. No one at all."

"Of course," said Ariadne. She pretended to sew her mouth shut.

I got down under my bed and reached for the hole in the mattress. The little leather-bound book fell out in my hands. I placed the latest pages inside it gently. If only there were a way to put it all back together again.

Ariadne sat up. "Can I look at it?" she said.

I handed it to her, watched her run her fingers over the letters on the cover. It felt so strange, seeing someone else hold the diary. But it seemed right, somehow. Ariadne was a true friend, I was sure of it.

I expected her to open up the book, to read the letters that Scarlet had written to me. But instead she just held it out, reverently, and then placed it back in my hands.

For once, luck seemed to be on my side.

That was, until we went down to breakfast, and all hell broke loose.

Chapter Seventeen

"SILENCE!" screamed Miss Fox. She slammed her cane down hard on a nearby table. "I will have silence, or none of you will be getting a single bite!"

Ariadne and I shared a fearful look as we sat down.

The rabble of the dining hall dissolved into uncomfortable quiet.

"Someone," Miss Fox said, pausing to glare at everyone, "broke into the kitchens last night. This morning the door was found unlocked and there were candles and saucepans spilled all over the floor."

Blood rushed to my face. I felt as though the words 'IT WAS ME' were engraved into my forehead. I tried desperately to think of something else, something innocent. *Kittens. Fluffy bunnies. Dainty embroidery.*

"The culprit has gone through all the cupboards. So which one of you was it, hmm? Which one of you thought it was acceptable to break the rules in MY school?"

She started pacing around the hall, up and down the tables.

"There is to be NO leaving your rooms after lights out, do you hear me? If you need the lavatory, it can wait until morning. I will be making sure everyone stays in their beds, is that clear?"

I heard the swish of her cane as she walked behind me. *Oh no, oh no...*

And then she slammed her hands down on our table.

"I said IS THAT CLEAR, Miss Winchester?"

I clutched at my chest, convinced I was having a heart attack.

Penny looked up, the colour draining from her face. "Yes Miss," she muttered.

"Do you have something you'd like to share with the whole school? Because it must have been important if you felt the need to say it while I was talking about a Very Serious Matter."

Penny's eyes had gone wide. "It was nothing," she protested. "We were just... wondering who could have done it. That's all."

"Are you sure it wasn't you, Miss Winchester?" hissed Miss Fox, pulling Penny up by the sleeve of her dress. "Were you confessing to your little friends, perhaps?"

Penny shook her head frantically. She looked like she was about to choke. Nadia and Josephine immediately looked the other way.

Miss Fox simply stood there for a moment, not saying a word, before gently lowering Penny back down to her chair. "Well," she said, "perhaps you can continue your wondering during your lunch hour, which you will spend in my office. Fifty lines of 'I will not talk while my betters are talking', I think. Understood?"

"Yes," Penny whispered.

"EXCUSE ME?"

"Yes, Miss!"

"That's better." The Fox turned to face the whole room once again. "You may continue with breakfast, but I hope you have all been listening carefully. Stay in your beds at night, or you will face the consequences."

"Yes, Miss Fox," we said in unison. I stared at my knife

and fork, determined not to act suspiciously. Ariadne grabbed my hand under the table and squeezed it gently.

What were we going to do now? If Miss Fox was going to be patrolling the corridors every night, well...

We'd been so stupid, not tidying up and locking the door behind us. Not to mention that our actions had got Penny into trouble. I almost felt bad about it.

Almost.

I sat in biology with my head in my hands. My emotions were scattered all over the place. Just when things seemed to be looking up, everything had come crashing down again. Quite literally, in fact.

Our biology teacher's name was Mrs Caulfield. She kept it written at the top of the blackboard at all times, which was a great help to me. I'm not sure if it was much use to anyone else, unless they were unusually forgetful.

"Today we'll be learning about anatomy," she said. "Please open your textbooks at page seventy-two."

Mrs Caulfield had handed out thick red books with the words 'Anatomy of the Human Body' on the cover. There was a picture of a happy-looking skull just underneath. How cheerful.

"I'll be back in a moment," said Mrs Caulfield. She was a white-haired woman who looked a little like a baby owl.

"I'll just go and get Wilhelmina."

She disappeared into the cupboard at the front of the room.

I glanced over at Ariadne, who was a few seats away from me. "Who?" I mouthed.

Ariadne shrugged and looked as puzzled as I felt. It was a relief to not have to pretend that I knew what was going on.

Moments later, Mrs Caulfield returned, wheeling a skeleton behind her. The thing was grinning at me, much like the skull on the front of my book.

How awful!

Mrs Caulfield picked up the skeleton's arm and made it do a mock wave. "Say hello to Wilhelmina, class. She has been helping me teach anatomy for many years."

About half the class joined in with greeting Wilhelmina. The other half, including me, just stared in shock.

"Now, as you can see from the height," continued Mrs Caulfield, "Wilhelmina was a young girl. In fact, she was a fellow pupil of yours who wished to donate her bones to the school. Aren't we lucky?"

Oh goodness. I thought I was going to be sick.

"There are two hundred and six bones in the human body. From the toes –" she leant down to point at the poor deceased girl's feet – "to the skull." It seemed to take her an age to bend back up again. "And someone has handily put a little catch in here..."

She flipped a metal catch and lifted the top of the skull.

I couldn't take it a moment longer. I ran out of the classroom and sank down outside the door, my heartbeat pounding in my head. I tried to stare out of the window and think about something else, but it was no use.

Scarlet, I thought. *Scarlet's going to be nothing more than bones.*

Tears ran down my face. I couldn't stop picturing skeletons and coffins and graves. All those dark things I'd tried so hard to keep from entering my mind.

I sat and sobbed into my arms, until I felt a hand on my shoulder.

"Mrs Caulfield sent me to see if you were all right," Ariadne said gently.

I wiped my cheeks with my sleeve. "Oh, Ariadne," I said, tapping my fist against my forehead. "I'm supposed to be acting as normal as possible. But how can I, when nothing about this whole thing is normal?"

She blinked at me.

I sighed deeply. "I've made myself look crazy again, haven't I?"

"Was it the skeleton?" she asked gently.

"Yes," I replied. "It was just so creepy, you know..." I gave Ariadne a meaningful look, hoping she would realise what I was saying.

Ariadne nodded and her kind eyes sparkled with understanding. I felt like hugging her.

"We'll find out what happened to Scarlet," she whispered, as she helped me stand up. "I promise."

I managed a weak smile. Peering through the small window back into the biology classroom, I saw that Mrs Caulfield was using a ruler to point at various parts of the skeleton. *Just breathe,* I reminded myself. *It's no different to looking at a picture in a textbook.* And I went back into the room, with Ariadne following behind me.

I was thoroughly relieved when our biology lesson ended and I could say goodbye to Wilhelmina. I'd been so caught up in everything that I'd almost forgotten I had ballet class after lunch. I felt relieved to be going there next. Apart from Ariadne, Miss Finch seemed to be the only person at Rookwood who cared.

I was the first to arrive.

"Good afternoon, Scarlet," Miss Finch said, curtseying.

I mirrored her actions. "Good afternoon," I echoed.

"Have you had any more late-night excursions?" she asked in a mock whisper.

"Oh no, I wouldn't dream of it."

"Of course not." She smiled at me. Had she heard about

the kitchen incident? I supposed she must have done. Miss Fox had shouted about it loudly enough for the whole school to hear.

Footfalls thudded down the basement stairs – the rest of the class were arriving.

Miss Finch began playing some music on the piano. It was a beautiful, lilting melody that seemed to wash away all my upset from earlier. I stood and listened to it in a daze, letting the tune flow through me.

That was until Josephine pinched me on the shoulder. "Wake up, Scarlet!" she hissed.

To my surprise, Miss Finch actually noticed this and stopped playing. "Miss Wilcox, keep your hands to yourself, please."

Josephine pulled a face at me and walked off.

We went through our usual ballet class routine. But when we got to *allegro*, Miss Finch said, "I think you girls are ready for something a little more advanced, don't you? I want to see who can perfect a *grand jeté*. And I mean perfect. Your legs should form an exact straight line, a one hundred and eighty degree angle. Come on –" she clapped her hands – "let's see what you can do."

We lined up at the side of the room as Miss Finch began to play some simple music. "One at a time, please," she said.

A petite blonde girl went first, darting across the space

and leaping through the air.

"Wonderful, Margaret," said Miss Finch. "But watch your back leg, it's trailing a little."

A few more girls followed, none of them managing the perfect angle, but all good efforts. Then it was Nadia's turn.

Her *grand jeté* was good – her turnout just right, the height was perfect. When she'd finished, she gave us all a smug smile.

"Well," said Miss Finch, "you're very nearly there, Nadia. But your movements are too mechanical. You need to be more fluid. Do it with passion!"

The smugness melted from Nadia's face and she said, tartly, "Why don't you show us yourself then, Miss?"

Everyone gasped. We all knew you should never talk to a teacher so disrespectfully.

Miss Finch stood up, slowly. Then she said, "I believe you all know that I can't." She calmly pointed to her crippled leg. "I can demonstrate simple things, certainly. But a *grand jeté* is beyond me."

"Then why are you teaching us?"

Miss Finch looked as though she'd been slapped. Her cheeks flushed pink and tears shone in her eyes. Her mouth moved silently.

The old Ivy wouldn't have stepped into this situation. She would've tried to fade into the background, avoided the conflict. But I knew one thing for sure – that Scarlet would never stand for it.

I stepped forward. "Leave Miss Finch alone, Nadia."

Nadia turned to face me, her arms folded and eyes dark under her long lashes. "Why, Scarlet? If she can't dance properly, she cannot teach, can she?"

"Of course she can. Maybe *you* just weren't paying enough attention?" And I instinctively prodded her in the chest.

"Hey, get away from me!" She raised an arm, and I ducked, expecting a blow.

"Girls, enough," said Miss Finch. "Enough!"

I backed away from Nadia, her eyes still glaring at me.

"Nadia, I want you to leave my studio, right away. Write an apology to me or I will send you to Miss Fox. You can come back when you are ready to take your lessons seriously."

Nadia started to protest, but Miss Finch looked stern. The girl dropped her arms to her sides with an exasperated sigh, and then stormed out of the room.

Silence followed. None of us dared to speak.

"I'll do it," I said, suddenly. "The *grand jeté,* I mean. I'll show you what I've learnt."

Miss Finch nodded, and she started to smile again. "Go ahead."

I was nervous, but perhaps my late-night practising had done me some good. I danced across the room and, as I jumped, I tried my hardest to get everything right. I thought I even heard my legs click as they flew into the splits.

As I reached the mirrors on the other side, relief washed over me. I turned around and saw that Miss Finch was clapping gently. "A very noble effort, Scarlet," she said. "You haven't quite got the height yet, but you've got the passion. And your turnout was perfect."

She turned back to the other girls. "Next, please!"

Chapter Eighteen

"I've been thinking about the diary," said Ariadne without looking up.

It was evening, and after another unsatisfying dinner and lukewarm bath I'd returned to our dorm room with a towel wrapped around my damp hair. My friend was sitting on top of her perfectly made bed sheets, chewing a pencil and balancing an open exercise book on her lap.

I shut the door quickly behind me. "Careful!" I replied. "You never know who might be lurking."

"Oops!" Ariadne went wide-eyed. "Sorry. I didn't think."

I smiled at her and went to sit down at the dressing table. "It's all right. So, did you have an idea?"

"Well, sort of. Maybe. A bit. More of a question."

I sat for a minute, waiting for Ariadne's brain to untangle itself. The page she was writing on was covered with scribbles and doodles.

"We're looking for the number one of something, right? So that could be anything that there's more than one of..."

I glanced at my reflection in the dressing-table mirror, watching my twin's image staring back at me. I almost couldn't believe that Scarlet had been clever enough to come up with this whole thing. Then I felt guilty at that thought and brushed it out of my mind. I shouldn't think so lowly of my sister. After all, I was the one who'd blown the entrance exam. "There's usually method in her madness. Maybe something that has numbers written on it."

Ariadne paused, gripping her pencil tightly. "Um... um... stables. No, we've had stables. Dorms. Office drawers." And then suddenly she cried, "Lockers!"

The pencil snapped in half. She looked at it with a baffled expression, as if not sure how it had happened, and then back at me. "Lockers have numbers on. Now, where are there lockers?"

I thought about it, as Ariadne began to write more things

down with the pencil stub.

The changing rooms by the gymnasium.

The ones by the pool.

There might some in the staffroom... and so on.

Wait, not the staffroom. I was pretty sure Scarlet wouldn't have hidden a top-secret diary page in the staffroom. She wasn't *that* stupid.

"The gym and the swimming pool," I said.

Ariadne nodded and clapped her hands together with glee, before realising that was perhaps a bit much. "Sorry."

"Don't worry about it. And... thank you, Ariadne. For your help."

"It's no problem," she replied. "Oh, I do love mysteries!"

As the bell signalled the end of classes the next day, Ariadne and I headed for the gymnasium. It was three o'clock and there were still plenty of girls milling about the corridors.

I hadn't been in these changing rooms before. They were through a pair of double doors to the right of the gym, and as we walked inside they appeared much the same as the swimming pool ones, all wooden benches and coat hooks. The room smelt of sweat and shoe polish.

Ariadne looked around. "There's no one here," she whispered.

"Then why are you whispering?"

"Oh," she said, a little louder. "Good point."

"We're only here to look for your socks, after all." I winked at her.

"Of course!" We'd decided it had to be Ariadne's hockey socks that we were 'searching' for this time.

The changing rooms had showers, through a little archway in the far corner. One of them was dripping steadily on the white tiles. The lockers stood nearby, a vast row of silver metal that looked like it had come from an army boot camp.

I weaved through the benches and faced the lockers. Each had a label on the front, bearing a printed black number.

Ariadne appeared beside me. "Number one," she said, pointing to the locker furthest to the left.

I darted over to it hastily, relieved to see a little key in its lock. I twisted it and the door opened...

Revealing an empty box.

I frowned. Well, it wasn't always a bad sign. I felt around the inside, the metal cool under my fingers.

Ariadne peered over my shoulder. "Maybe there's a secret panel or something?"

I shook my head. "I don't think so. Lockers don't really need secret panels." But I tried anyway, pushing on the back and the sides. It yielded nothing.

"Bother," she said. "Shall we go to the swimming pool, then? Unless you want to check all of them in here."

"Not really. Let's leave that as a last resort."

Outside the sky was iron grey and there was fine misty rain in the air. We walked past the rippling pool and over to the right where the squat changing rooms stood.

I was a little more worried about this. After all, it might be hard to convince someone – Miss Bowler or whoever else – that we'd come looking for Ariadne's hockey socks by the swimming pool.

Thankfully though, these changing rooms were empty at this time of day too. I made a beeline for the wooden lockers.

The numbers were painted on in faded black. Some of them had rubbed off completely, but it was still easy to locate locker number one.

Ariadne bounced up and down excitedly. "This could be it!" she squeaked.

But when I tried to open the door of the locker, I realised we had a problem – there was no key.

And it was locked tight.

Chapter Nineteen

I stood there for a moment, staring gormlessly at the empty keyhole.

"There's... there's no key," I said. "I can't open the door."

Ariadne pulled out a hair pin and tried it in the lock, where it promptly snapped. "Drat," she whispered. "I don't think it will work with these. Why did she take it, I wonder?" She went silent for a moment, but then cried out, "Of course! If she'd left the key in the door anyone could have found the pages, couldn't they? So she had to hide it. But where?"

I sat down on the bench opposite the wall, and Ariadne plopped down next to me.

"I don't know," I said. "Where's a good place to hide a key? I mean, Scarlet must have hidden it somewhere she knew I could find it. But I've searched our room completely, and a lot of other places besides. There has to be a clue we're missing."

Ariadne nodded.

We both sat there for a moment, gazing at the lockers. And then Ariadne had an idea. "We should check the ones around it," she said, jumping up. She twisted the tiny brown keys in numbers two, three, four and five. As each door popped open, she peered inside.

I watched her, darting about. Ariadne had seemed so shy and easily flustered when I'd first met her, but clearly she was as sharp as a tack.

"Aha!" she said suddenly. She'd retrieved a tiny strip of paper from the top of locker four, directly to the right of number one. There was a bit of tape on the top from where it had been stuck down.

"Is it from the diary?" I asked.

"Um, maybe... It's only one sentence." Ariadne's face went a bit pale. "It says 'I've swallowed the key'."

"What?! That can't be right." I started pacing up and

down on the wet tiles. "It doesn't make any sense! She does want me to open the locker, doesn't she?"

I was getting a bit hysterical. Ariadne was looking at me as if I were about to explode.

"It must mean something else. Or someone else wrote it! What if someone else wrote it and it has nothing to do with any of this?" I grabbed the piece of paper out of Ariadne's hand. It was definitely Scarlet's handwriting. I would recognise it anywhere. Tears pricked my eyes, bitter and angry.

My friend seemed a little scared, but she didn't say anything about it. Ariadne had started reading the words over and over, her eyes going back and forth. I looked at her, breathless. *Calm down,* I tried to tell myself. *We need to find the truth. Together.*

Then, a moment later, she spoke again. "I-I think you're right, Ivy. It does mean something else. You'd never get to the key if *she'd* actually swallowed it. So what else could swallow a key?"

I thought about it. "An animal? Ugh, that wouldn't be easily retrievable either."

Ariadne nodded. "Right. So this must be a metaphor. She's hidden it in something."

"Then why not just say that?" I snapped in frustration. "Why be so cryptic and say it was swallowed unless it was actually swallowed?"

Neither of us had an answer. We traipsed back to our room, defeated. I remained silent the whole time, while Ariadne spouted out mad ideas.

"A drawer! A hollow tree! A button box! A... lavatory!"

I raised an eyebrow at her. "You think Scarlet might have put an important key in the lavatory?"

"Maybe not," said Ariadne sadly. "But I'm running out of suggestions."

On Friday afternoon, I got a reply to my letter from Aunt Phoebe. The post was given out at the end of assembly, with Miss Fox watching over us like a hawk. I wondered if she read all of them beforehand.

I dashed back to the dorm with my letter, hoping that my aunt had cottoned on to my plight. The familiar sight of her slightly wobbly writing made me smile wistfully as I unfolded the letter. It read:

Dearest niece,

Your letter finds me well, though I do miss you terribly. I had quite forgotten to water the plants, but I'm sure they will live. That is what rain is for, of course!

You say you have found out something interesting about goldfish? You must tell me all about it sometime. I'm glad to hear that you are learning things. I think Rookwood School will be very good for you.

Will you be able to return for the Christmas holidays? I shall look forward to seeing you then, though I must remember to get enough coal – I'd better write that down somewhere. In the meantime I hope you can continue to get on with your studies. One day you might even become a doctor like my Arthur. I am so proud!

With all my love,

Your aunt

Phoebe Gregory

I sighed. My aunt was the kindest of souls, but a little lacking in the brain department. Another spark of hope dwindled away.

On Saturday, I spent every chance I got looking into various containers, in case they contained one of the tiny brown keys. I looked in every drawer, every nook and cranny. I even searched around the lavatories, though certainly not in them.

I was beginning to think I would never be able to solve this clue. What could swallow a key if it wasn't alive?

That very question was crossing my mind as I walked past the biology classroom on Monday afternoon. I was on the way back to our room to get changed for ballet, but when

I passed the little glass window in the door I froze completely.

Because there was something in the cupboard of that room.

And it had certainly *once* been alive.

There were only a few other girls nearby, chatting amongst themselves, and soon they would all be in their classes. I waited for them to pass and then peered into the biology room. It appeared to be empty, unless Mrs Caulfield was in the cupboard too. I supposed I could always think up a burning question about biology to ask her.

I opened the door cautiously. The room smelt of Bunsen burners and a faint odour that might have been dead frog. I wrinkled my nose.

The cupboard door at the side of the blackboard was wide open, though there was no light coming from within. Did I really want to go in there with that... thing? *Oh, Scarlet!*

I approached the cupboard and pulled on the light switch. The bulb made a fizzling noise as it came to life, but then moments later exploded.

I ducked, shielding myself from the glass. *Wonderful*, I thought. *Just wonderful. Now we're going to get a lecture from Miss Fox on the misuse of light bulbs.*

At least nobody else could have heard the small explosion from outside of the classroom. I stood up and brushed myself off. I could just about make out huge shelves in the darkness, lined with jars full of strange, greenish liquid with parts of long-deceased creatures floating in them.

And, in one corner, the white teeth of Wilhelmina grinned back at me.

Come on, Ivy. This was not terrifying. I only had to go into a dark cupboard with a real-life skeleton and stick my hand inside its mouth.

Gulp.

I went in, treading carefully to avoid the broken glass. The only sound was the faint ticking of the classroom clock. Wilhelmina appeared to be trying to outstare me, her empty eye sockets filled with shadow. I breathed as steadily as I could, and forced myself to stand face to skull with the deceased girl.

There were little rusty hinges on the skeleton's jaw, the same as those Mrs Caulfield had used to open up the top of the skull, and wires holding the whole thing together. I shuddered.

I stretched out my shaking hands towards it. *You're doing this for Scarlet*, I told myself. *Just think about getting the next page of her diary.*

I unhooked the clasps on the little hinges and, wincing, tugged on the skull's jaw. It yawned open with a horrible creaking sound. Wilhelmina clearly hadn't made any trips to the dentist in recent years.

And, as it opened, I saw it – a glint of something darkly metallic in the shadows of the gaping mouth. Quivering terribly, I put my hand in to retrieve it.

I tried to ignore the feel of the teeth scraping on my wrist and the rising urge to scream.

And then... there it was. The tiny brown key.

"Oh thank you thank you thank you," I whispered. I wasn't sure if I was thanking Scarlet, or even Wilhelmina, but I was thankful all the same.

I quickly closed up the jaw, hoping it wouldn't be too obvious that I'd been in there. But a crunch under my foot reminded me of the exploded light bulb. *Oh well.*

I stowed the key safely in my pocket and dashed outside. A quick glance at the clock told me I had already missed ten minutes of ballet class.

"Could you pick somewhere a bit less awful to hide your clues next time, Scarlet?" I muttered under my breath as I hurried through the corridors.

Unfortunately, I had a feeling that things were only going to get worse from now on.

Chapter Twenty

Miss Finch's piano playing came to a halt as I scurried into the room. She stood up. "Where have you been, Scarlet?" she demanded.

Everyone turned from the *barre* to look at me. I felt my face flush red. "Sorry, Miss Finch."

"Scarlet," she repeated, "I didn't ask for an apology. I asked where you'd been."

"I…" I hadn't thought I would need an excuse; Miss Finch was usually so lenient. So I decided to borrow the excuse my teacher had used herself. "I was feeling unwell."

I could see the disappointment in her eyes. "Is that so," she said. "You've missed the warm-up and the *barre* work. I suggest you get on with those by yourself."

I nodded and sat down to lace on my shoes. Nadia stuck her tongue out at me, but I ignored her.

"Oh," said Miss Finch, "and see me after class."

"Yes, Miss Finch," I replied miserably.

I remained at the side of the class doing stretches and simple moves while the rest of the girls danced. I hated to watch other people dance when I couldn't join in – it was like being in a cage. Every second, I longed to leap through them and spin pirouettes until I was dizzy. Anything but being left out.

I felt guilty for being late and angry at myself, but at least I had the locker key. For the first time, it occurred to me that if I managed to find all the diary pages and work out the truth about what had happened to Scarlet, then maybe I could escape this ghastly place.

When the bell rang for the end of the day, I stayed where I was, watching my reflection in the mirror. I saw everyone else curtsey and file out of the room at the edge of my vision.

When the last girl had left, I watched as Miss Finch approached me in the mirror. "Why did you lie to me, Scarlet?" she asked softly.

The way she said it put me even more on edge. She hadn't spoken like a teacher. She'd spoken like someone who'd been genuinely upset that I'd lied.

I clenched my fists as I turned to face her. "Because I can't tell you what I was really doing," I replied.

Oh no. Why had I just said that?

She raised her eyebrows at me. And then, unexpectedly she asked, "Was it important?"

I nodded, not daring to open my mouth in case it said anything else stupid.

"All right."

All right? I'd been expecting to have to write lines at the very least.

"Just don't do it again. You're one of my best students and –" she gave a weak smile – "you know I have *problems* with some of the others."

"Yes, Miss."

At first I presumed she was talking about Nadia, but there was something in the way she said it that made me think otherwise. Maybe there was a reason why Penny no longer took ballet.

"I'll be on time next lesson, Miss," I promised. And I meant it.

At the top of the basement stairs I pulled the door shut

behind me, and almost ran straight into the round figure of Miss Bowler.

"Slow down, girl!" she barked. "And don't slam doors. Were you born in a barn?"

"Sorry, Miss. No, Miss," I said.

I edged around her and walked on, slowly. I needed to get back to the changing rooms by Miss Bowler's horrid swimming pool and find out what lay inside locker number one.

Ariadne wasn't back from hockey when I got to our room. I pulled on my uniform and checked that the key was still in my pocket, its coldness reassuring to the touch. I tried not to think about the fact that it had spent the last few months inside a dead girl's skull.

I hurried back downstairs and out towards the swimming pool, a cold breeze swirling around me.

The changing rooms were deserted again, and they smelt even more of damp. There was a rack of the hideous woollen swimming costumes hung up to dry in one corner. The floor tiles were sopping, and I had to tread carefully as I tiptoed towards the lockers.

There it was. Number one.

Hadn't anyone ever wondered where the key was or why it wouldn't open?

I inserted the tiny brown key into the lock and felt a

flood of relief when it fitted. I twisted it and the locker door popped open.

My heart rate quickened. There was no tape this time, the pages were simply lying at the bottom of the locker.

After a quick glance over my shoulder, I picked them up and began to read.

Dear Diary,

I don't trust Violet. Not one bit. She touches all my things, I'm sure of it. I think she might even read what I write in here. Can you believe it? Everyone knows you should never read someone else's diary. Even Ivy wouldn't read mine, and she's my twin.

I've kept this diary under my pillow, but I saw Violet standing near it when I came back from the lavatories today. So I've decided I need a better hiding place for it. I'm sure I can think of something to thwart her!

Sometimes I think she might be following me. When I'm alone I often hear footsteps, see curtains moving when I turn around. I went for a bath yesterday, and when I walked out with sopping-wet hair she was <u>right there</u>. Just standing outside the door, staring. "What are you doing?" I said, and she replied, "Waiting for a bath. Is that a crime?"

But I didn't believe her for one second. Her eyes are like a snake's.

I'm not even sure if it's just me that she's spying on. I see her making notes on things all the time, in strange places. Once I thought I saw her snatching glances at an old photograph, but she hid it before I could look.

One day I will find out what she's up to, I promise you that!

This Violet girl was sounding more sinister by the minute. I read on:

Dear Diary,

Today in English literature, everyone started giggling when I walked in. They tried to stifle it but it spread like wildfire. "What?" I demanded. I could feel their eyes burning into me. It was only when I turned to the blackboard that I understood why.

Someone had drawn a horrible caricature of me with the teacher's chalk. The name 'Scarlet Grey' floated around the figure's head in scratchy letters. They'd given me bulbous eyes and straggly hair, and a tongue that poked out of a too-big mouth.

I looked... dead.

I didn't have to ask who'd drawn it. I went straight up to the desk where Violet and Penny sat smirking. "You're not going to get away with this," I said.

Penny laughed, twirling her hair bow with her fingers. "I think we already did," she replied. So with all my strength, I tipped their stupid desk over on to the floor. Their inkwells smashed and spilt ink blossomed black across their books. Ha!

Violet screamed at me, and that was when Miss Brown walked in. I saw her eyes widen in fury and I just had to run.

I think I was intending to go to the roof but for some reason my legs carried me down to the ballet studio. Miss Finch was there, reading a book in between classes.

She asked me what was wrong and I... I just cried. I know! I never cry! I felt like a complete baby. I told her that Violet won't leave me alone, that she follows me everywhere and goes through my things. And I told her all about the horrible tricks she and Penny have pulled on me. Miss Finch was sympathetic, and she said that she knew how it felt to be picked on. She said I should try to ignore it.

Miss Finch is different from all the other teachers here. She didn't even reprimand me for running out of class.

I will try to ignore Penny and Violet, but I'm not sure I can go on much longer. If they do one more thing to me, I'm going to snap. Honestly.

I crumpled the edges of the paper under my fingers. It was becoming hard for me to read these entries. Poor Scarlet!

I blinked away stinging tears and checked overleaf, hoping for a clue. I wasn't disappointed. But this one was just as obscure as the others and hastily scribbled:

Search on your knees.

Well, I had done a lot of that already, hadn't I?

I wished that I could talk to my twin, just for a moment, just once more. Sitting down on one of the slightly damp benches, I tried to *think* as loudly as I could, hoping that Scarlet would somehow send me a sign. That she would tell me what had really happened between her and the other girls. That she would unravel this whole mystery for me.

That she would tell me I wasn't alone, and she was waiting for me on the other side.

But there was nothing. Only silence.

I ran back to my room alone.

Chapter Twenty-One

I flew through the door of room thirteen and collapsed on to my bed. Ariadne was embroidering a cushion and she almost jumped a mile when I ran in. I buried my face in my pillow, wishing everything would just go away.

"Ivy?" said Ariadne, keeping her voice low.

"Go away," I said, though it came out completely muffled.

I heard her footsteps as she walked over and then tried to peel the pillow off my face. I pulled it straight back down again.

"I don't want to talk about it," I said.

"But... we have to go down for dinner soon," she replied, poking me gently in the shoulder. "What's wrong? Is it about the diary? Did you get a beating again?"

"Nothing. Yes. No." I rolled over and stared at the ceiling. "It's complicated," I said finally.

Ariadne sat back down on her bed with a thump. "Can I help?" she asked.

I sighed and didn't reply. But a few moments later I began to feel guilty about ignoring my only friend. I propped myself up on one elbow and tried to paste a reassuring expression on my face. "I just need to... gather my thoughts a bit. You go to dinner without me, I'm not hungry."

Ariadne's mouth dropped open. "You can't miss dinner! You'll starve!"

I shrugged, or at least the best I could shrug while lying down. "Don't worry about me. I'll see you later on, all right?"

She didn't look convinced. "If you say so," she said, her eyebrows drawn.

It was only later that I realised Ariadne was probably worried about going to dinner alone.

I put the latest diary entry on my chest and took a deep breath, trying to sort through the things I knew.

One. Scarlet was dead. And though I hated to even think it, someone might have killed her.

Two. Penny and Violet both hated Scarlet, and Violet seemed to have been spying on my sister.

Three. Violet was missing – or at least not at the school any more.

But I still had more questions than answers. Why was Violet spying on people? Why would anyone hurt my twin? And why was Miss Fox covering the whole thing up?

That was probably the part that was hardest to fathom – Miss Fox demanding that I impersonate my twin. And how on earth did Scarlet *know* that this would happen?

What worried me further was how easy it was becoming to keep up the charade. Absent-mindedly wringing my sheets through my fingers, I thought long and hard about how I'd been acting recently. I was getting better at being Scarlet. It was coming all too naturally for me.

I knew deep down that I was still more Ivy than Scarlet, but maybe this was getting to me too much. I just *hoped* I wasn't being as reckless as she was.

My stomach started to grumble. I was being stupid, not eating. I shouldn't punish myself.

I got up and hid the diary pages inside the mattress. The hall clock told me I was only twelve minutes late for dinner. Even if I'd missed the main meal, there was still the chance of pudding.

*

When I arrived at the dining hall, breathless and panting, there was still one girl left in the dinner queue. I darted through the tables and fell in line behind her.

Miss Fox's head snapped around to look at me. *Drat!* Just because there wasn't a rule against being late for dinner, it didn't mean she couldn't invent one in order to punish me.

The girl in front looked back and smiled at me – it was Meena Sayani. "Chicken surprise!" she said, holding out her plate.

I glanced at it. It looked ordinary to me, though perhaps a little too pink. "What's surprising about it?"

"That it's not in a stew," she replied with a wink. I grinned. Meena was certainly preferable company to her sister.

I took my plate and sat down heavily next to Ariadne. She was prodding her food with a fork and apparently hadn't noticed I was there until now.

"Oh, I— Scarlet! You *did* come!" She looked suddenly relieved.

"Yes, sorry. Couldn't miss this lovely... meal," I said, a bit too sarcastically.

The chicken came with potatoes, peas and cold gravy. It wasn't the worst thing I'd ever tasted, but it certainly wasn't the best.

Mrs Knight gave me a half-hearted withering look from across the table. "Now, girls," she said. "Eat up, please.

Remember your manners."

"Yes, Mrs Knight," we said in unison.

"Freaks," someone whispered.

I didn't even bother looking to see who it was. I already knew it would be Penny or one of her gang.

As I chewed my dinner, the noise of everyone else around me filtering through my ears, I just kept thinking – what had Penny got against my twin? It had to be something to do with what happened with Violet, I decided. But what could it be?

My train of thought soon derailed, and I began to wonder why Miss Finch never seemed to be in the dining hall. Many of the other teachers ate here, though I assumed that was because they had to supervise us rather than that they enjoyed the culinary delights. But I had never seen her...

I was barely paying attention when Penny stood up with her plate and walked towards me. Then everything seemed to happen in slow motion.

First, she tipped the cold sloppy leftovers from her plate into my lap. I heard her say 'whoops!', as if she'd forgotten how her own hands worked.

Ariadne gasped and hid her face.

Penny's friends giggled helplessly.

I stood up, my dress dripping with food, and slapped her as hard as I could.

Penny screamed and clutched at her cheek. The whole

hall went silent. I shook out my stinging hand.

"*Whoops!*" I echoed.

"Well, really!" said Mrs Knight, her mouth gaping.

Unfortunately, Miss Fox had lightning-fast reactions, and almost instantly I felt one of her claw-like hands clamped around the back of my neck. With the other she had hold of Penny's arm in a vicious grip.

"Both of you. My office. Now," she said, in a voice that could melt steel.

"Miss, she hit me!" protested Penny.

Miss Fox's dark eyes filled with storm clouds. "I said *now*, Miss Winchester."

We were both dead meat.

As Miss Fox marched us from the hall, a commotion started up. First only whispers, then I heard unmistakable gasps: "She slapped her!"

Oh my goodness, I slapped Penny. Why did I slap Penny? What was I *thinking*?

Penny didn't say a word, though her face had gone some odd shades of red and purple. I wasn't sure if it was from where I had hit her or from sheer embarrassment.

Miss Fox pushed us into her office. I reached for a chair, but she smacked my hand away. "You do not deserve chairs," she snapped. "If you behave like animals, you will be treated like animals. Sit on the floor."

I sat, cross-legged. The sad stuffed dogs looked down on me from the walls. I prayed that I wasn't about to become a piece of taxidermy.

Penny sniffed. There were red lines raised on her cheek. "I'll get my dress dirty," she said in a whiny voice.

Miss Fox gave her a look, and she dropped to the floor next to me. "Ugh," she muttered.

As if you can talk, I thought. The whole front of my dress was damp and sticky.

"SILENCE!" screamed Miss Fox, so loudly that I swear the Chihuahua on her desk rattled.

We both sat bolt upright.

"Now, Miss Winchester," she said, bending over so that her face was level with Penny's. "What made you think it was acceptable not only to waste your dinner, but to tip it on to another pupil?"

"She deserved—" Penny began, but once she'd started she realised what a bad idea this sentence was. "I don't know, Miss."

Miss Fox stared at her, until Penny's teeth started to chatter and her nose threatened to drip. Then Miss Fox fixed me with the same death glare.

"And you, Miss Grey. Do you think I tolerate acts of violence in MY school?"

Replies that Scarlet would make ran through my head.

It's not your school, it's Mr Bartholomew's. Wherever he is.

You seem to be fine with violence when you're the one inflicting it.

You seem to take pleasure in it, in fact.

But I didn't have a death wish. I had to say something...

There was a *whooshing* sound and suddenly there was a line of stinging pain blazing across my face. *Ouch!* Miss Fox had just hit me with her cane. I clutched at my cheek.

"WELL?" she said.

"No, Miss Fox," I said. My teeth were gritted and it came out as a low hiss.

She stood up straight. "Both of you are despicable. I've a good mind to write to your parents and –" she paused as her eyes fell on me and swiftly changed tack – "No, I think we need a more severe punishment in this case."

Penny gulped and wiped her nose with her sleeve.

Miss Fox began to pace up and down. I got the feeling she was stalling while she tried to think of the most horrible thing she could do to us. Either that or she just enjoyed prolonging our suffering, which was incredibly likely.

After what seemed like several hours, she snapped her fingers and turned to face me. "So," she said, "there is obviously some quarrel between you two?"

I wasn't going to say a word, but Penny took this as a golden opportunity. "Oh yes, Miss. She's up to no good. I don't think she's ever been up to good!"

Miss Fox nodded and then her face stretched into a grin not unlike the one worn by Wilhelmina.

"I think, then, you will thoroughly enjoy spending every night this week cleaning the dining hall after dinner, TOGETHER, since you both made such a mess."

"Oh no," I whispered.

Penny slammed her fists down on the floor. "But Miss..." she started to protest.

Miss Fox's cane swished up and stopped just short of Penny's horrified face. "Don't you 'But Miss' me! You will do as I say. And just for that, you can sit next to each other in every lesson as well."

My mouth dropped open.

"And if I hear ONE SINGLE COMPLAINT from either of you, you will be cleaning up after breakfast and lunch as well. Do I make myself clear?"

I nodded solemnly. Penny wisely followed suit.

"I'm sorry, what was that?" Miss Fox cupped a hand to her ear dramatically.

"Yes, Miss Fox," we both said.

"Good," she replied, and walked back over to her chair. She sat down heavily, took a fountain pen from the mouth of the unfortunate dog on her desk and began to write something down in a notebook.

Penny turned and glared at me. There were tears in her eyes and her face was a mess.

You started it, I mouthed at her.

She gritted her teeth and her nose wrinkled in disgust. But as I watched, her expression began to turn hopeful.

"Does this mean... we aren't going to get a beating?" she asked.

Miss Fox didn't even look up from her desk. "Oh no," she said. "You're still getting a beating. But since you wasted my time, I'm going to waste yours."

"What?"

"I have some paperwork to do for the next hour. You can wait until then."

Penny and I glanced at each other in shared horror, momentarily forgetting our mutual hatred.

"Where should we wait?"

"Right there. In silence. Or else."

Chapter Twenty-Two

By the end of that night I would have sworn I was an expert on every inch of Miss Fox's office. I'd counted every canine photograph (nineteen) and every stuffed dog (eight of the hideous things). There were seven pens and three pencils on the desk. Thirty books on the shelves. I could go on.

Penny spent most of the time rocking back and forth and muttering things under her breath. At least I had spent my time productively, or gathering useless knowledge, depending on which way you looked at it. After an hour, she looked like a nervous wreck. I would have guessed that she'd had beatings before, but maybe not. Miss Fox gave her twenty lashes across her knuckles, and she sobbed and whimpered the whole time.

I told myself that if I could just act like Scarlet, if I could stay strong, I would be all right. So I stood there, fists clenched as the cane bit into my skin. I knew it would sting for days.

And all I could think was: *get through this for Scarlet*.

Afterwards, the Fox waved us out of her office without even a second glance. I was expecting Penny's usual bile as soon as the door slammed shut, but she was gone in seconds, running towards the stairs in tears.

As I traipsed back to room thirteen, I contemplated the rest of my punishment. *A whole week with Penny – ugh*. Making us both suffer the pleasure of one another's company while at the same time preventing us from getting up to anything individually. Miss Fox was pure evil.

I opened the door gingerly, my hands feeling like they were on fire. It didn't help when, a few moments later, Ariadne jumped on me.

"OH MY GOODNESS! I can't believe you *slapped* Penny, oh my goodness, what happened? Did you get punished? Oh, it was BRILLIANT! You should have seen the look on her *face*!"

Despite everything, I had to laugh. I gently pushed Ariadne away. "It was pretty good," I said, croakily.

Ariadne finally appeared to realise that I was feeling a little fragile. "Did Miss Fox keep you in her office this whole time?"

"Yes," I coughed, showing her my hands. Ariadne fetched a glass of water from her bedside table and placed it on mine. I shuffled over to my own bed and sank down on to the mattress. "Thanks."

The water tasted like heaven, my mouth was so dry. Ariadne waited patiently until I'd drunk most of the glass and was able to talk again.

"Miss Fox is a fan of cruel and unusual punishment."

Ariadne sat down on her bed and grimaced. "Was it scorpions?"

I blinked at her. "No." Then, "Perhaps worse. I've been sentenced to spend extra time with Penny."

Ariadne's face summed up exactly how I felt. "Oh, yuck."

"Precisely."

There was a knocking on the door and the matron peered around it. "Lights out now, girls," she said, sternly.

"Yes, Miss!" squeaked Ariadne. I got the feeling she was really keen to avoid any rule breaking, lest she be ordered to follow Penny around too.

The matron nodded her approval. "Sleep well," she said,

and pulled the door shut.

Ariadne breathed out. "Phew." Then, as she climbed into bed, she turned to me. "Wait a minute," she whispered. "Did you find the next bit of the diary?"

I got up and opened the door of the wardrobe, obscuring Ariadne from view. "Yes," I sighed. I pulled out my nightgown and began to get changed for bed.

"Oh gosh, what did it say?" asked Ariadne from behind the door.

"I almost forgot about it," I said quietly, as I got into bed.

Ariadne was looking at me expectantly. "Go on, then – where did you find the key to the locker?"

"I figured out what could 'swallow' something without being alive." I cringed a bit as I turned on to my side. "It was in Wilhelmina, the skeleton."

"Ooooh," said Ariadne.

"I had to stick my hand inside her skull. Then I went to the locker and found the pages."

"Yes, and...?" said Ariadne, wide-eyed.

"Apparently this Violet girl was spying on people. She was always acting suspiciously, going through Scarlet's things, making notes and being all secretive. And then the next entry was about Violet and Penny drawing a picture of her on the blackboard. It was... it was grotesque."

Suddenly Ariadne pointed a finger at me and gasped.

"What if it was *them*? What if they did something *terrible* to her? You don't think...?"

"Hold your horses," I whispered. "We still don't know what happened to Scarlet. Or Violet. But I wouldn't put it past them to do something bad." Ariadne's words troubled me.

"Was there a clue at least?"

"Something about 'searching on our knees'."

Ariadne sighed. "That could mean a lot of things."

I didn't say much more. My hands were killing me and I was exhausted, but I knew I wouldn't be able to sleep.

Scarlet, the diary, Penny, Violet.

All of it had to be connected, somehow.

When I woke the next day, it was bright outside the thin curtains and I felt pleasantly warm. Then the events from the day before came crashing over me like a tidal wave. Suddenly I was filled with nausea and dread.

I got dressed in a daze and followed Ariadne down to breakfast.

"I hope there will be no trouble today, ladies," said Mrs Knight, as we sat down in our usual seats.

"We'll be on our best behaviour, Miss!" replied Ariadne eagerly.

Penny walked in, looking a complete state. Her copper

hair resembled a birds' nest, and her face was deathly pale. She didn't even bother to glare at me as she passed.

In history I sat at my desk next to Ariadne, the same rose-scented one that had belonged to my twin. Madame Lovelace looked up from the book she was reading. "Scarlet, Penelope," she said. "I've been told you two are to sit together. You –" she looked at Ariadne blankly – "Missy, please swap places."

Ariadne looked flustered and started picking up her pile of books. I watched as she shuffled over to Penny's desk. Penny sat down next to me with a thud.

About twenty minutes into the lesson, a piece of paper flicked across on to my desk. I frowned. Then I looked at Penny. She was staring at her exercise book rather too intently.

There, in blotchy blue ink, were the words:

YOU ARE DEAD

Penny didn't speak to me for the next few lessons, thank goodness. But her note lingered in my mind, looming and threatening.

At least she can't come with me to ballet, I thought, as I ran to my dorm room to get changed. When I got there, Ariadne was sitting on her bed, pulling on her hockey socks.

"I don't want to go," she moaned.

"Go where?" I asked.

She motioned to her outfit. "Hockey. It's a nightmare. Why couldn't they just let me play croquet?

"Can't you change to something different? Have you asked?"

She nodded sadly. "They said I'm stuck with it until the end of term. I'm not sure if I'm going to have any legs left by then!"

Poor Ariadne! "Maybe you'll get better at it," I said.

Her only response was to stick her tongue out as she picked up her shoes and began lacing them on.

I shivered as I walked into the ballet studio. "It's getting colder in here," Miss Finch said, as I passed her. "You'd better start warming up as quickly as possible."

I walked over to the *barre* with the other girls and began the exercises. I was in the middle of practising my *développé*, my leg stretched high in the air, when Miss Finch appeared behind me in the mirror. She was looking at me strangely. "That's perfect," she said. I smiled, and she smiled back, but there was a trace of uncertainty in her expression.

At the end of the lesson, we lined up and curtseyed for Miss Finch. She waited until the majority of the class had left the room and I was on my way out, and then suddenly asked,

"Can you stay back for a minute?" gesturing at me.

I went over to where she sat at the piano stool. She remained silent until absolutely everyone had left and I heard the door at the top of the stairs bang shut.

"That was some good work today from you, Ivy."

"Thank you, Miss," I said.

And then my mouth dropped open.

"I-Ivy?" I stuttered. "What? I... Who's Ivy?"

Miss Finch waved a hand dismissively. "I know you're not Scarlet, dear girl. You're far better behaved, for a start. You like ballet for the sake of ballet, not because you yearn for fame and fortune. You can do your *développé* perfectly, which Scarlet could never get right. She told me about her twin, so... that's you, isn't it? You're Ivy."

I dropped to my knees in front of her. "Please," I begged, "please don't tell anyone. No one's supposed to know."

Miss Finch tipped her head on one side. "What's all this about? Where's Scarlet?"

Tears threatened to roll down my cheeks. "She's dead," I whispered.

Her expression warped from confusion to pure shock. "Are you serious?"

I nodded.

"How did it happen?"

"I don't know," I sobbed. "That's why I've got to stay

here and find out. And I can't tell anyone who I am or else she'll—" I slammed my mouth shut.

"Ivy, is someone forcing you to act like Scarlet? Because whoever it is..." Suddenly, Miss Finch pushed herself to her feet, leaning heavily on the piano. She clenched her fists tight. "Oh, don't tell me. I think I know *exactly* who."

Chapter Twenty-Three

I could barely believe what had just happened. I thought I'd been so careful to act like Scarlet, untidy uniform and all. I'd even slapped Penny! But as I dashed away to get changed for dinner I saw suspicion in the eyes of every person I passed.

If Miss Fox found out that I'd let the cat out of the bag, she'd kill me. Or, worse, make me spend the rest of my life with Penny.

I could tell that Miss Finch had more to say, but I feared staying a moment longer in her presence. *She knew.*

At the dinner table I felt as if my brain had tied itself in hundreds of knots and I hadn't the faintest idea how to untangle it. I left my soup for so long that it turned cold.

Ariadne kept poking me until I spooned some into my mouth. "You'll need all the strength you can get for cleaning up with Penny after this."

I groaned and almost dropped my head into my bowl. That was the last thing I needed today.

A shadow fell over us and I turned around to see Miss Fox standing behind me. "I hope you haven't forgotten about your duties this evening," she said.

"No, Miss," I said begrudgingly.

She tapped me lightly on the shoulder with her cane. "Good."

"Oh dear," said Ariadne.

Miss Fox walked over to the dinner ladies, and though I couldn't hear what was being said I was pretty sure she was telling them not to clear up this evening. Wonderful.

I stayed in my seat as everyone finished eating and began to leave the hall.

"See you soon," said Ariadne sympathetically, picking up her bowl and taking it over to the pile.

Not long after, the room was empty except for Miss Fox, Penny and me. The dinner ladies had retreated into the kitchen and closed the wooden hatch.

"Right, *girls*," said Miss Fox. "I want these tables clean enough to see my face in. And the floor too."

Penny grumbled but I just nodded.

Miss Fox slammed her cane on the floor, making both of us jump. "What are you waiting for? Get started!"

"Yes, Miss," we chorused. The dinner ladies had left out brooms, dustpans and brushes and cleaning cloths. Just looking at them brought a sudden wave of exhaustion over me. The dining hall was *huge*.

Miss Fox's heels clicked away through the big double doors, and I picked up a cloth and started scrubbing the nearest table.

Moments later Penny appeared next to me. "I can't believe you got us into this mess," she sneered.

My mind told me to ignore her, but the part of me that was acting like Scarlet couldn't let that slide. I threw the cloth down and looked her straight in the eye. "*I* got us into it? You were the one who chucked the contents of your plate on me!"

Penny snorted like a horse. "You didn't have to hit me, though." She gestured at her bruised nose. "And besides, we all know you deserved it."

Oh yes, the mysterious thing *I* had apparently done wrong. I sighed. I couldn't keep fighting battles that Scarlet had started.

"Look, Penny, let's just get on with the cleaning, shall we?"

Penny had clearly been expecting an argument but I wasn't going to give her one.

To my surprise, she didn't say anything in retaliation. She simply began flicking crumbs off the table with her cloth.

She remained silent as we worked our way around the tables. My arms were aching a little, but it wasn't too bad, not compared with my stinging hands.

I picked up a broom and began sweeping up all the small bits of discarded food that littered the floor. Penny suddenly stopped right in front of me.

"I meant it, you know," she said, staring at me, her face unmoving.

"Meant what?"

"The note."

Ugh. I'd almost forgotten about that.

"I'm not just going to let you get away with everything." Her bottom lip was shaking.

I narrowed my eyes at her. "Excuse me," I said, and continued my sweeping.

I tried to hide the fact that Penny had shaken me. I definitely wasn't comfortable with being alone with her, even with the clatter from the kitchen where the dinner ladies and cooks were washing up.

"Oh for goodness' sake!" she exclaimed at one point, throwing her broom to the floor. But when I looked over she just glared at me, lifted the handle back up and started again.

What felt like hours later, I stopped for a rest against the wall. The tables were pretty clean by now and we'd swept all the dirt into neat piles on the floor. It had grown dark outside the tall windows. I was just about to finish emptying my dustpan when Miss Fox returned.

She swiped a finger along the table nearest to her and then inspected it. I remembered that she had done exactly the same in Aunt Phoebe's kitchen, and I felt a rush of homesickness.

"Hmm," she said. "I suppose that's adequate. You will do better next time, I trust."

I stared at her blankly, refusing to react. The room was almost spotless and she knew it.

Penny, however, was not so quick on the uptake. "It took us *ages*, Miss!" she said from behind me. "My hands are practically bleeding!"

Miss Fox's eyes lit up. "Wonderful! Hard work builds character. If you do twice as much tomorrow, you'll have *twice* as much character. Won't that be grand?"

Penny slumped down into the nearest chair and stared at her feet.

"May we go now, Miss?" I asked, having tipped the final

pile of dirt into the dustbin.

"Yes," Miss Fox snapped, and marched out of the room without saying another word.

As I went to leave, I noticed Penny was still sitting down, her head in her hands. I didn't have to, but for some reason I felt obliged to say something. "Bye?"

"Get lost," she replied, without looking up.

Lost?

I was already lost.

I spent a considerable amount of time soaking my aching body in the bath that night. Eventually the matron knocked on the door and told me I had to get to bed. I didn't protest.

When I got back to our room, Ariadne was already asleep with the lamp still on. I smiled down at her. She always looked so peaceful, and fell asleep so easily.

I really should have tried to get some sleep too, but instead I got down under the mattress and retrieved Scarlet's diary. I sat down on the floor and spread out the pages in order. No matter how many times I looked at them, I never saw anything new.

I stood up and peered at myself in the dressing-table mirror. The face looking back at me was blank and tight-lipped, not revealing anything.

Sighing, I gathered up the pages again. I placed them

back inside the leather-bound book, stroking my hand over the raised letters, and then returned the diary to its hiding place.

The curtains fluttered, and I realised that the window was open and the door ajar, creating a breeze. I shut both, before changing into my nightgown, turning off the lamp and finally, exhausted, falling into bed.

Just as I was slipping into sleep, a thought swam through my mind: *If Miss Finch knew who I really was, there was no reason why she couldn't tell me more about what had happened before Scarlet's death.* But before I could chase that thought, it was carried away and the current of sleep pulled me under.

The next day Penny's behaviour was even worse than usual. She was constantly trying her best to get me into trouble in every lesson.

In Latin, she kept dropping her pen and flicking ink everywhere each time the teacher's back was turned. "It was Scarlet, Miss!" she said and I got a rap across my sore knuckles.

In biology, she kept elbowing me, making my handwriting into a spidery mess. Mrs Caulfield ordered me to do ten lines of 'I must write neatly' after class.

In home economics, she knocked a whole bag of flour off

the table and then screeched and flung her hands in the air. It was Ariadne who had to clean it up, and me who had to go and scrub my dress in the washroom.

But the strange thing was that Penny didn't seem to be joking with her friends any more. As I was leaving the cookery room Nadia nudged Penny and said, "I hope you don't catch the freak pox off *her*."

Penny, however, didn't join in with the jibe. "Shut up, Nadia," she said, shrugging her away.

Nadia's face turned sour. "What is wrong with you?" she snapped.

I left them to their bickering. I had a ballet class to get to.

That was when things took a turn for the strange – or perhaps, more accurately, the *stranger*. Miss Finch was away again, only this time there was no Miss Fox ordering us to swap to swimming. Instead there was merely a note on the piano telling us to get on with some floor work on our own.

Afterwards I headed back to our room in a cloud of disappointment. Ariadne was already there, optimistically trying to read and sew at the same time. She seemed a little less bruised than she usually was after hockey.

"I just avoided contact with the ball as much as possible," she said with a cheerful grin when I asked about it.

I laughed half-heartedly and sat on my bed.

"Oh," she said, putting down her book. "I had an idea while I was out on the hockey field! You know the chapel?"

"Yes, what about it?"

"Scarlet said something about getting on our knees, right? Well, I could see the chapel from the hockey field... and I just thought – praying! Knees! So maybe we should check the pews?"

I nodded, as the idea took hold; it was about the only place we *hadn't* searched yet. "Ariadne, I think you might be some kind of undiscovered genius," I said.

"Maybe I am!" Ariadne jumped off the bed, knocking her sewing on to the floor. I reached down and picked it up. It said 'BEST FRIENDS', with cross-stitched flowers all around it. I put it back on her bed gently. A warm glow spread inside me and pushed away the gathering gloom. I'd never had a best friend before, unless you counted Scarlet.

Ariadne was already reaching for her satchel. "They can't tell us off for going to church, can they?"

The chapel was on the east side of the school, surrounded by a meadow on one side and the playing fields on the other. There was a small graveyard next to it, presumably from when the school building had been a manor house in previous centuries. Without warning, my imagination populated it with dead schoolgirls. I shuddered as we waded through the uncut grass.

As with most churches, the door was never locked, though it did have a large iron ring handle that was heavy to lift.

I went in first and looked around. "Empty!" I whispered, beckoning Ariadne to follow.

Our footsteps echoed off the walls as they hit the clay floor tiles. It was surprisingly bright inside, as light poured through the stained glass.

"Where shall we start?" Ariadne whispered excitedly. There wasn't really any need for us to talk in hushed voices, but it seemed the right thing to do.

I looked along the pews. They all had tiny numbers in front of each seat. "Number thirteen, perhaps? It was Scarlet's favourite."

Ariadne ran over and started counting along the row. "Oh," she said. "There is no thirteen. It goes from twelve to fourteen. They must have thought it was unlucky."

"But not unlucky enough for them to inflict it on our bedroom!" I thought about it. "Number four, then?" The other hiding places had followed that pattern. But the fourth seat was right at the front, with nowhere to conceal a diary entry. "Hmm, how about where we sit on Sundays? Scarlet would have had to sit in the same place, wouldn't she?"

I found our pew and slid into it. It was identical to every other one in the chapel, with its hymn books and embroidered kneeling mats, each bearing the name of the person who had sewn them. "Let's look underneath."

We both got down on our hands and knees and crawled the length of the pew. It was surprisingly dusty and Ariadne couldn't stop sneezing, which made me giggle. I clamped my hand over my mouth, trying to dampen my laughter and keep the dust out.

There was no sign of anything taped under the wooden seat or on the floor, as far as I could see. "Anything your end, Ariadne?"

She sat up and stuffed her handkerchief under her nose. "Nothing here."

Hmmph. I took a seat on the pew. "Let's check these," I said, gesturing at the hymn books and kneeling mats.

"Oh yes," said Ariadne, somewhat muffled by the handkerchief.

I was in the place where I normally sat, seat twenty-four. "I'll take the kneeling mat, you take the book." I handed it to her.

The prayer mat featured a cross-stitch picture of a shepherd with his flock, and was clearly the work of a less than perfect student. On one of the sides, there were big stitches that were more than a little wonky. I peered at them closely.

"This could be it," I whispered. "Maybe there's something

inside." I began picking at the stitches. Ariadne was flipping through the prayer book, which she dangled upside down and shook to see if anything came out – but nothing did.

I felt a little strange to be destroying a prayer mat, even if it was for a good reason. "Forgive me, Father, for I have destroyed your kneeler," I said.

Ariadne smiled. "I'll bring a needle and thread and sew it back up on Sunday."

When I'd finally unpicked all the bad stitching, I could stick my hand inside the cushion. It was full of stuffing and... paper?

I pulled it out. Oh, just ordinary packing paper, put in there to make up the rest of the bulk.

Ariadne's face fell. "No writing?" she asked.

"No, but..." I put my hand back in and began pulling out more of the balls of paper. I threw about ten on to the floor until suddenly, "Aha!" The next scrunched-up ball had scrawls of ink all over it. *Diary pages!*

Ariadne squeaked and clapped the tips of her fingers together in an attempt to make less noise.

I shuffled up the pew, unfolding the diary entry. It read:

Dear Diary,

You won't believe what has happened. It all started when I went to get my hairbrush, the silver-backed one with Mother's initials, and it wasn't there. I tore the room apart looking for it, and then I realised – it wasn't lost. Violet had taken it. I just <u>knew</u>.

Well, I wasn't going to let her get away with it this time. I sat seething through my first lesson, just waiting to get my hands on her. In home economics, my chance finally came. At first I was only going to yell at her, but then she pulled out Mother's hairbrush from her satchel and started brushing her hair with it. The letters E.G. were plain to see on the back. When she looked around, I was glaring daggers at her, but she just laughed and tossed her curls.

Mrs Weaver was at the back of the class helping someone else cut their fabric, so I took my chance. I went straight over there and demanded that Violet give me back the brush. She nudged Penny and giggled, so I grabbed her arm.

"Give it back now," I said. She blinked her stupid eyelashes at me and said, "Scarlet, what are you talking about? It's <u>my</u> brush." Then Penny chimes in: "Yeah, Scarlet, it's hers. Leave us alone, you freak!"

So I picked up Violet's satchel and pulled out the hairbrush myself. And that's when Violet squealed, "Miss! Scarlet stole my hairbrush!"

I lost control. I grabbed a pair of pinking shears from their desk, took hold of a bunch of Violet's pretty locks and snipped them right off. They looked like dead leaves as they curled in my hand. Violet started shrieking as if I'd murdered her.

I got a caning and I had to go to bed without dinner. But it was worth it.

Violet is going to regret the day she picked Scarlet Grey for an enemy.

Oh dear.

Ariadne was reading over my shoulder. She motioned at me to turn the page.

Dear Diary,

I think I might have finally broken Violet. She has stopped taunting me, stopped speaking to me at all. I've not noticed her lurking around me any more, and my things in the wardrobe and drawers look untouched, which hasn't happened in ages. It's almost unnerving.

A few times she hasn't even come back to our room at night, and when I wake up in the morning her bed doesn't look slept in. If the Fox catches her, she'll really be for it.

Her hair still looks a mess. It's so short now that she looks like a boy. It serves her right.

Penny on the other hand has completely flipped. She doesn't stop screaming at me, and in ballet the other day she kicked me so hard that she left a bruise. In today's lesson she was constantly tripping me and trying to get me into trouble.

Miss Finch finally got angry with her and made her do lines, but she still didn't get thrown out of class. I'm going to get back at her for this — I promise. Soon she'll be leaving me alone too.

Ariadne looked at me. "This doesn't sound good," she said.

I frowned. "I wonder what Violet was really up to? Wait, there's more." I flattened out another of the paper balls.

Dear Diary,

I've done something terrible. I shouldn't have done it, I know, but I was just so angry.

Ariadne gripped my arm tightly.

"What did you do this time, Scarlet?" I whispered.

Penny shoved me back down the basement stairs after ballet. No one else saw, because I was last in line and Miss Finch had already left a little early for a doctor's appointment. When she reached the top of the stairs, Penny turned and hit me in the chest. I tumbled over and hit every stone step on the way down.

I sat at the bottom and cried for a while, knowing no one was there to see me. But when I climbed back up, I saw Penny's pale blue hair bow lying on one of the steps. And that gave me the idea.

I feel so ashamed. I went to the caretaker's cupboard and found a mallet. And I smashed up Miss Finch's piano. I thought about everything Penny and Violet had done as I hit it, and I just felt more and more angry. Then when it looked sufficiently battered, I threw down the mallet and casually dropped Penny's bow on the floor beside it. Then I went straight to Miss Fox in tears and told her that Penny was responsible. That I'd seen her doing it, and how she must be cross with Miss Finch for punishing her. Miss Fox was <u>livid</u>.

So now I'm sat here in my secret place on the roof, alone. I'm imagining the look on Penny's face when Miss Fox gets to her.

But then I think about Miss Finch and how she must feel about the piano, and it makes me feel sick to my stomach.

I hope I haven't gone too far this time...

Ariadne and I sat in silence, just staring at the pages. I'd always known that Scarlet was reckless, but this?

Despite everything, a tiny voice in the back of my mind whispered, *At least it wasn't something worse.*

"No wonder Penny hates you," Ariadne piped up.

I nodded. "And now she's banned from ballet class. Although... maybe she doesn't know that Scarlet was responsible. She might just be suspicious."

I felt certain that we were closer than we'd ever been

221

to the truth about my twin, but all we had were puzzles upon puzzles.

Dejected, we both stood up. I concealed the pages inside my dress as usual. We had to get back to our room now, as it wasn't long until dinner.

I hung the unstitched kneeling mat back on its hook and hoped no one would notice the damage. Outside the chapel, it had started to rain. We ran at full pelt around the back of the school, our feet crunching on the gravel. I prayed that the pages would stay dry, as it was the deceptive kind of rain that soaks you quickly.

Ariadne tugged open a small back door and we both hurried in, our hair already sodden.

"Goodness," she spluttered, wiping water from her eyes.

We plodded up to our room, both still reeling a little from Scarlet's last diary entry.

"Goodness," Ariadne repeated, as she shut the door behind us. I wondered if she'd forgotten the rest of her vocabulary, until she said, slowly, "Your sister was quite the character, wasn't she?"

I rolled my eyes. "You could say that." I sat down at the dressing table and pulled the crumpled and slightly damp pages out of my dress.

Ariadne smiled, but she looked distracted. Her world was so simple, but now darker things were beginning to seep in.

"It's half an hour until dinner time," she announced.

"All right." I sighed, not looking forward to being on clean-up duty again. "Let me just put these pages away." I flattened them out on the top of the dressing table. The ink had run a little, but they were still readable.

I got down on my hands and knees, crawled to the bed and slipped underneath on my back. I stuck my hand inside the mattress, feeling for the leather book with 'SG' on the cover.

I wriggled my hand about, scratching myself on the springs and knocking out even more stuffing than I had before. And I grasped hold of... *nothing*.

The diary was gone.

Chapter Twenty-Four

"Ariadne! Did you move the diary?"

"No," she replied, her voice sounding far away. "Why would I?"

My breathing sped up. I pulled myself out from under the bed, my hair damp and my dress covered in mattress stuffing. "It's gone!"

Ariadne looked horrified. "Are you sure? Maybe you forgot to put it away properly last time?"

I grabbed my pillow and pulled off the case, but nothing fell out. I dragged all the blankets and sheets off my bed.

I hurled open the wardrobe doors and pulled out every single drawer and...

"Ivy, stop," whispered Ariadne.

But I wasn't listening. I had to find the diary. It had to be there.

Ariadne soon gave up trying to calm me down and started going through everything as well.

It wasn't long before there were clothes, books and bed sheets all over the floor. I sank down in utter despair.

The diary was gone. *Taken*. The only bit of Scarlet that I had left. The book that held all her secrets. All *my* secrets.

"My sister..." I said, numbly staring at the wall. Ariadne sat down next to me and tried to put her arm around me, and a second later I started sobbing. "Who would do this? Who would take her diary?" I shook my head, the tears running down my cheeks. "No one even knew it was here!"

Ariadne started pulling on her hair. "I don't know!" she said, looking on the verge of tears herself. "I didn't tell anyone, I swear!"

I don't know what came over me then, but I grabbed hold of the collar of her dress and pulled her towards me. "PROMISE ME! Promise me you didn't tell a soul!"

"I didn't!" she whimpered. "Ivy, please!"

I let go of her quickly, as if my fingers were burnt. "Sorry, sorry," I murmured. "Oh, Ariadne, what are we going to do?"

My friend was shaking. She leant back against her iron bed frame. She looked like a mouse again, like the first time I'd seen her.

"Who would've done this?" I repeated. "If Miss Fox got hold of it then I'm finished. Or what if—"

I'd just thought of one other person who hated me more than anything. Who hated *Scarlet* more than anyone.

I jumped up and hurriedly wiped the tears from my face. "That *witch*." I said quietly.

Ariadne put her hand over her mouth. "Ivy, goodness, what is it?"

"It was her. *She* took the diary. It has to be. I'm going to kill her." I clenched my fists.

"Who did?"

"Penny," I spat. I was shaking now too, but with rage. I would not let her get away with this.

I ran for the door and threw it open, oblivious to Ariadne's attempt to hold me back. I marched down the corridor, no doubt looking completely wild. I suddenly realised I had no idea which was Penny's room. So I just started walking backwards and banged on every single door I passed. Girls poked their heads out and stared at me.

"What on earth are you doing?" asked Anna Santos from room eight, her brown hair half-combed. I ignored her and carried on, until as I passed one door, Nadia Sayani's face

226

appeared. "Yes?" she said haughtily.

I grabbed hold of her and swung her out against the wall.

"Where is Penny?" I demanded.

Nadia wriggled and tried to kick out at me. "How should I know?" she said. "She's not even talking to me!"

Just then Anna called out, "I think I saw her go upstairs."

I'd never been to the top floor and I'd presumed there wasn't anything up there. "Are you sure?"

"Yes, yes!" she said, looking a bit terrified. "Go and see for yourself!"

I took one last look at Nadia and then dashed off towards the staircase. My feet pounded on the wooden boards. The space narrowed as I went up, until my head was almost reaching the ceiling, and it got brighter as well. At the top of the stairs there was a big slanting window hatch, flecked with drops of rain. It was open a crack.

I climbed the steps up to it and pushed the window open wide. Sure enough, I could see a silhouette out on the flat of the roof. *Penny*.

I scrambled outside. The rain had eased off but it was still coming down in gentle sheets. This part of the roof was wide, surrounded by chimney stacks and sloping sides. I tried not to look down as I walked, grateful for my good balance. The dark tiles were slick with rain.

Penny was facing away from me, staring out over the fields

and trees. There was something in her hands. I couldn't see it properly, but I didn't need to.

I clenched my fists. "PENNY!" I screamed, as I neared her.

She spun around, her wiry hair whipping in the wind, her blue bow hanging limp from her head. She held up the diary like some sort of trophy. "Are you looking for this?" she said. "Who even are you, *Ivy*?"

I reached up to try and grab it from her, fearing that the loose pages were about to fly out over the school grounds at any moment. But she had a vice-like grip, and she quickly shoved it behind her back.

"All I wanted," she said, "was to find something that would humiliate you. Or maybe prove that I shouldn't have been the one thrown out of ballet class. But this?" She shook her head. "This is priceless!"

I tried to calm down, to breathe evenly. "How did you find it, Penny? Did someone tell you? Did you make them?"

She glared at me. "Maybe you should shut your door properly, and make sure no one can see into your room."

"You conniving little…"

"Ha! You think I'm any worse than you? Wait until I tell Miss Fox what you're up to!"

I pushed my rain-soaked hair out of my face. "I think you'll find she already knows, actually."

Penny's eyes flickered with doubt and she took a step

backwards, towards the chimney stack behind her. "What?" she said. "She knows you're not Scarlet?"

"Oh yes," I said. "Miss Fox knows everything. You've got nothing. Scarlet's not here any more. Only me." I moved towards her, my palm outstretched, as if approaching a wild animal. "Just give me the diary back, Penny. I'm serious."

She looked away from me and shook out her wet hair. "You're bluffing," she said flatly, staring out across the rooftop.

I kept my eye trained on her right hand, which held Scarlet's leather-bound book. I prayed it wouldn't be permanently destroyed by the rain. "Penny, please. You can't get me into trouble with it, because the whole thing was Miss Fox's idea. And you can't prove the whole ballet thing was Scarlet's fault, either, can you?"

Of course she couldn't. Those pages were back in room thirteen.

"You expect me to believe that the Fox knows about all of this? Then tell me why it says that you can't let her know. I read the whole thing!"

It was then that I heard a voice shout my name through the rain and the wind.

Ariadne was climbing out of the hatch on to the rooftop. "Careful, Ariadne!" I shouted to her, but I wasn't sure if she heard. She came towards me unsteadily.

I looked back at Penny.

"Your pathetic little mouse friend knows about this too? This is a complete joke..."

"Listen, Penny,"

"NO, YOU LISTEN! Everyone thinks they can make a fool out of me! Well, I'm not having it any longer!" She spat her words into the rain. "*I* deserve to be the one at the top of the ballet class!"

I stood there, staring her in the face, hearing Ariadne panting behind me. I saw Penny falter on those words. "You're *envious*," I said, not quite believing it.

"Of course I'm envious! I was always the best ballerina, better than Nadia, better than you and your horrid sister! And it was all taken away from me."

There were raindrops on her face, but I could tell there were tears there too. Penny's eyes were red and raw. My anger was getting the better of me, but I couldn't rein it in, not even at the sight of her crying. "You're a mean and selfish brat! You don't deserve anything!"

Penny tossed the diary at her feet and dived at me screaming. She knocked me on to the soaking tiles, slamming my back into the ground, and started trying to slap me. I gritted my teeth and used all my strength to throw her off.

Ariadne shot past me, reaching down for the diary, but she skidded and went careering into the chimney.

I watched in horror as her head hit the blackened stone and she slumped on to the tiles. "Ariadne!" I cried.

I scrambled towards her, but Penny was suddenly standing over me, grabbing hold of my hair. "How do you like it?" she yelled. She kicked me with the side of her shoe. "Liar! Just like your sister!"

My scalp stung but I still tried to pull away from her to get to Ariadne. I could see a trickle of blood making its way down the side of my friend's head.

"Oh no," I whispered.

Penny loosened her grip. She'd spotted that Ariadne lay with her hand outstretched just by the diary.

Time froze. Penny stumbled.

And I lurched forward.

Chapter Twenty-Five

"Ariadne, wake up!" I called.

Seconds later, Ariadne's eyelids fluttered and she started to moan.

Thank goodness, she was alive!

"Ariadne, are you all right?"

"Yes," she whispered.

As relief flowed through my veins I snatched up the diary. I clutched it to my chest and rolled over, gripping it tightly. I came perilously close to the edge of the flat part of the roof, the dizzying sight of the ground below spreading out before me.

Penny glared at me as I crawled back to safety, her breathing ragged. "So you have the stupid diary! What good will it do? I know all your wretched secrets now."

I struggled to my feet. I was completely soaked through. "But I have your proof," I said.

"That means nothing!" she shrieked. "I can still tell everyone who you really are!"

Just then, Ariadne coughed and said something so quietly that I couldn't hear it over the wind.

"What? What did she say?" demanded Penny.

"Trade," Ariadne repeated louder, her voice croaking.

Keeping an eye on Penny, I moved over to my friend and crouched down next to her. "Trade what?" I whispered.

Ariadne put a hand to the cut on her head, around which it was rapidly turning purple, and groaned a little more, but then she said, "The proof. We have the proof that Penny was framed. You could tell Miss Fox."

Penny's ears pricked up. "What are you suggesting, mouse?"

I glanced at Ariadne, realising what she meant. Although I couldn't show Miss Fox the diary, I could still own up to what Scarlet had done. Penny would get to dance again and... and I would probably be banned from class instead. Oh.

Ariadne turned to me and whispered, "Ivy, we've got no

choice. She's going to tell everyone."

I cried out in frustration, then turned to Penny. "It's true," I said. "We have a page where Scarlet admits what she did to you. If you swear..." Penny rolled her eyes. "If you SWEAR on your life that you will keep your mouth shut, I'll own up to it."

I held my breath.

Penny clenched her fists and suddenly sat down on the roof. She stared out at the grey world around us, as if her anger and despair had summoned the rain clouds. "All I ever wanted was to be a ballerina. For people to love me."

"Well, then you and me... and my sister... we're not so different, are we?"

"I'm not like you," Penny growled.

But then, after a pause, she seemed to come to a decision. "All right. You tell them that you – that Scarlet – smashed up the piano. But if they don't let me dance again, the deal's off."

I looked at Ariadne, who was still clutching at the side of her head. The rain swept more trickles of crimson blood down her face.

"Fine," I said. "It's done."

I reached down and helped Ariadne up. She staggered and put all of her weight on my arm. I clutched the diary in one hand, and we made our way carefully back across the roof, as the wind lashed our hair across our faces. Penny didn't even move as we walked past her.

"Are you all right?" I asked Ariadne again.

"Oh, perfectly fine," she replied. But seconds later her eyes rolled back into her head and her legs went from under her. I lifted her up and carried her through the window hatch.

At the bottom of the stairs, a crowd of girls had gathered, all talking excitedly. Their eyes went wide as they took in the sight of me and Ariadne, now swaying on her feet, both soaking wet and one of us bleeding.

Nadia stood there with her hands on her hips. "What were you doing up there?" she demanded. "Where's Penny?"

"Go and see for yourself," I replied impatiently.

"I'm not going up there in this weather!"

The other girls nodded in agreement. "We'd catch our death!" Ethel snapped.

I didn't have time for this. "Look, I need to get Ariadne to the nurse! Can you please move?"

"For goodness' sake..." started Nadia, as I pushed past her. Ariadne moaned and stumbled along with me. The crowd parted.

"I'll help you," said a small, shy-looking girl, as she pulled Ariadne's other arm over her shoulder.

"Thanks, Dot," murmured Ariadne.

I let Dot lead the way along the corridor and down a small

stairwell where there was a door with a discreet red cross painted on it. She knocked gingerly and when there was no answer I banged on it with all my strength.

"What on earth?" said the nurse, appearing from behind the door. "What's all this racket?" She had her dark brown hair pulled back in a bun, and thankfully a friendly face. She wore a pocket watch and a name badge that read 'Nurse Gladys'.

"My friend... fell down the stairs," I lied. "She hit her head."

Nurse Gladys thought quickly. "Let's get her lying down. What's your name, dear?"

"Ariad... ne... 'm perfectly... 's all right," said Ariadne. Her speech was getting more slurred. We helped her up on to the metal bed. There were two more identical beds in the large room, along with a sink, a desk covered in first-aid paraphernalia and a giant metal medicine cabinet with a hefty padlock. The whole place smelled of disinfectant.

"Goodness, you're soaking wet!" said the nurse.

"We just came in from outside. But Ariadne forgot something and tried to run back for it. She slipped on the stairs." The lies were coming easier to me now.

"Looks like she has concussion." Nurse Gladys got a wet cloth and started dabbing at the cut on Ariadne's head, making her wince. "Did she hit something sharp when she fell?"

"Um... the corner of the skirting board, maybe?" I replied.

She nodded thoughtfully. "Let me get this cut cleaned up, dears. Then she's going to need a lot of bed rest."

I sat down on a metal chair next to Dot. "Ariadne's a nice girl," she said, sniffing. "She stopped me getting hit by the ball three times in hockey."

"Calm down," said Nurse Gladys. She wrung out her cloth and then reached for some cotton wool. "She'll be right as rain in no time."

Dot sniffed again. I gave her a reassuring smile and took her hand. "You're right. Ariadne's a good friend," I whispered. She squeezed my hand back.

We stayed there for about ten more minutes as the nurse saw to Ariadne and gave her something to make her sleep. "You girls get back to your rooms. You can come and see your friend again tomorrow. I'll write this down in the accident book."

Reluctantly, we left the nurse's room. I prayed that Penny had been keeping up her end of the bargain since we left her on the roof.

Back by the dorms, the crowd still hadn't dispersed. The other girls were standing around talking, all thoughts of dinner apparently forgotten. I darted into our room and hid the diary at the bottom of the wardrobe, not wanting to risk it until I knew if Penny's offer was genuine, and I hoped it would dry out quickly. Then I went back outside and joined the crowd.

A booming voice called out over the rabble, "What's the meaning of this? You should all be in the dining hall!"

Miss Fox. Just what I needed.

There was a great flurry of "sorry, Miss!" as everyone flowed towards the stairs. Miss Fox was standing there with her hands on her hips.

"You, Miss Grey," she said, pointing at me. "Have you been up to something?"

"No, Miss," I said. "Ariadne fell down the stairs so Dot and I took her to the nurse."

"Hmmph." She ran her gaze over my bedraggled state and looked skeptical, and for a moment I was terrified that she'd demand the truth. But she only said, "Dining hall, now. And no more trouble."

I shook my head no, but of course there *was* going to be more trouble to come. I was going to have to admit to what Scarlet had done to Miss Finch's piano, and face the consequences.

As if to remind me, Penny appeared, absolutely soaked through – even more so than myself.

"Miss Winchester, you look like a drowned rat!" said Miss Fox. "Go and get changed. You too, Miss Grey! You can't come to dinner looking like that."

I glanced over at Penny as we walked back to our rooms. She made a gesture at me – opening and closing her hands. A book. A *diary*.

A simple reminder that she could send my world crashing down at any moment.

Chapter Twenty-Six

It was strange sleeping in room thirteen without Ariadne. It reminded me of when I went to live with Aunt Phoebe, the first time I'd ever spent a night without Scarlet. I shivered in my sheets and tears welled in my eyes.

Dinner was no less awful, especially since I had cleaning duties with Penny to look forward to. She kept to the other side of the room, though, and didn't say a word. Nor would she look me in the eye.

Things seemed brighter the next day, even with the impending doom of owning up to Scarlet's misdemeanour hanging over my head.

I visited Ariadne in the nurse's room. She was propped up on pillows and had a white bandage wrapped around her forehead, but her eyes were bright.

"Are you going to do it?" she whispered. "Own up to the piano smashing?"

I nodded. "Of course. I have to."

I spent all of ballet worrying what Miss Finch would say when she found out. Every time she praised my dancing, I felt a jolt of anxiety.

I silently cursed my reflection in the mirror. In my head, Scarlet stuck her tongue out at me.

I was shaking by the time I got to the Fox's office. I wondered if she would even believe me. And as for how I was going to explain how I knew anything about it...

I knocked softly on the dark wooden door. Seconds later it swung open and I found myself looking up at the Fox's unpleasant face.

"Yes?" she said impatiently, staring over my head.

"I need to confess to something," I said.

"Aha!" she said triumphantly. "Why doesn't that surprise me? A wicked miscreant like yourself..."

"Not me." I shook my head. "*Someone else*."

Miss Fox raised her eyebrows and stepped to one side.

"In," she said.

I sat down on the chair, thankful I wasn't being punished just yet.

"Right." She had shut the door behind us and was now standing over me. "Pray tell me what *someone* has done."

"It's about the... unfortunate incident with Miss Finch's piano."

Miss Fox straightened up. "I recall it. Miss Winchester was duly punished."

"But it wasn't Penny, Miss. It was my sister." I lowered my voice for that last part, despite the closed door. "She got angry with Penny and tried to frame her..."

"Preposterous!" Miss Fox slammed her hand down on her desk, and the surrounding dogs wobbled. "How could you possibly know this? You weren't even attending the school then."

Thankfully I'd been up half the night working on my responses, so I knew what to say next.

"Scarlet wrote a confession." I pulled the sheet of paper from my pocket. Not a diary page, but a brand-new confession, carefully crumpled. "I found it in our room and... I thought that if I came clean and told you, Penny might leave me alone."

Miss Fox looked dubious, but she held out her hand. "Show me."

242

To the untrained eye, my handwriting was very similar to Scarlet's and I'd tried to make the confession seem as much like my sister's work as possible. I'd described her fierce rivalry with Penny, her desire to be the only one in the limelight. I'd written it as though she was proud of herself and took all the credit. Exactly what Miss Fox would expect.

"Stupid girl," said Miss Fox, shaking her head as she folded the paper up and put it away in a desk drawer. "This is exactly the sort of reckless nonsense that child would get up to." She gazed down at her Chihuahua pen holder, absent-mindedly tapping a nail on its snout. "If only I hadn't already punished Miss Winchester for this. And told her parents..." Suddenly she looked up at me sharply. "Not a word about this to anyone, you hear?"

I stood up. "But is Penny going to be allowed to join the ballet class again? Will you have to kick me out?"

Miss Fox just waved towards the door. "Get out," she said. "You can both do your *dancing*. I'll tell the Winchesters their precious daughter is innocent after all. Perhaps they'll make a grateful donation to the school."

I felt like collapsing to the floor with relief, but I still worried about what would happen when Miss Finch found out. I'd already come close to losing Ariadne, I didn't want to lose the only other person who seemed to like me. I'd seen the way she sat at her piano, that peculiar sadness that surrounded her as she played. She must have been really hurt by what had happened to the previous one.

I hovered at the edge of the office. "I'm... glad I told the truth," I said.

Miss Fox glared at me. "I can always change my mind and give you another caning," she snapped. "And if this will sort things out – I don't want to hear another word from you or Miss Winchester – I'll let you both off your punishment. Constantly checking up on you is a waste of my time. Do you understand, *Scarlet*?"

"Right, right, yes, Miss," I said.

I darted out of the door, leant back against the wall and caught my breath. I had done it. I had fooled the Fox and kept my end of the deal with Penny.

Now I could only pray that she would keep hers.

That evening as I sat alone in my room, I heard knocking outside in the corridor. I peered out – a younger girl had been sent to summon Penny from her room, no doubt to go and see Miss Fox.

Penny caught my eye as she headed for the stairs, then glanced away. I think she knew, or at least hoped, that I'd done what I'd promised.

I lay back on my bed and read *Dracula*, a book which I

had found hidden beneath Aunt Phoebe's bookshelves (she'd decided it was 'too racy'). Scarlet had always wanted to see the film with Bela Lugosi, but even the poster had been enough to frighten me.

I was so engrossed in my reading that I jumped when there was a knock on the door. I was hoping it might be Ariadne, released from the nurse's room.

It was Penny. She fixed me with a defiant look. "You did it," she said.

"Yes?"

"I didn't think you would."

I just stared at her. She stared back at me, and then walked away.

"You're welcome?" I called after her.

She turned to me, halfway to her room. "I'll keep my word. Just stay away from me, you hear?"

"Gladly," I muttered.

Ariadne returned the next day. Her head was still bruised and bandaged, but she seemed to be her old self again. "We've foiled Penny's fiendish plan!" she whispered to me at lunchtime. "Now we can solve everything!" She was so excited that she flicked her forkful of tinned ham across the table.

I sighed. "If only it were that simple. We still have

no idea where to look next." I took a sip of my too-hot tea and accidentally knocked over the milk jug. Clara and Josephine jumped and then gave me angry stares. It wasn't long before the giggles and whispers started up, and I was almost relieved to see Penny instigating them. As long as she wasn't revealing my secrets, she could say whatever she liked.

A while later, Ariadne and I were walking to our arithmetic lesson, when we turned a corner and met Miss Finch. She was wearing a long-sleeved blue dress instead of her usual ballet attire. She paused and then said, "Miss Grey, I've just spoken with Miss Fox."

If there was ever a moment to gulp, this was it. "You did?" I said quietly.

She gestured towards a little alcove in the corridor beside one of the tall glass windows. Ariadne gave me a fretful glance, but I waved her to carry on. I didn't want her to be late.

Miss Finch lowered her voice to just within my hearing. "She said... she said you admitted to smashing my piano." She paused. "Well, we both know that can't be true. Was it *Scarlet*?"

I exhaled and looked down at the floor. "It's true... she did it."

Miss Finch's eyes widened, but she said nothing.

"She was angry. Penny was bullying her, and she wanted to get revenge by framing her. I know it's no excuse. I'm sorry..."

The ballet teacher's eyes slipped off me, almost as if I had faded into the background. "I can't believe she would do such a thing," she finally said. I had never heard her sound so sad.

"I'm sorry, Miss," I repeated. "I'm sorry I have to apologise for her. I'm sorry for this whole situation. For everything." I sniffed hard to hold back the tears.

Miss Finch tapped me lightly on my shoulder. "It's not your fault," she said quietly, with sincerity.

I gave a weak smile.

Miss Finch looked frail as she stood there, leaning against the long window. "I can't believe it," she said again. "And Penny... wrongly accused. Goodness, I feel awful."

"Don't feel bad on Penny's behalf, Miss. She's done plenty wrong. Just not what you thought."

I almost told her about what Penny had done on the roof, then, but I dreaded to think that someone might be listening. "I need to get to class," I said.

She pushed herself up from the window and on to both feet, wincing a little as she did so. But as I turned to leave, she called after me, "Scarlet?"

I turned. It was surprising how quickly I could react to

that name these days.

"I'll find a way to help you."

I wasn't sure if anyone could help me now.

Chapter Twenty-Seven

Every time I walked past the door to Penny's room that weekend, she was in there practising and humming music. I decided to do some ballet practice too. Ariadne watched and clapped every time I did anything, even when I fell over after slipping on a sock.

As I was practising my *fouetté en tournant* for the hundredth time, Penny appeared in our doorway. I lost my balance and she clapped sarcastically. "You'll fit right in at the sideshow," she said. "I've heard they're auditioning for a new dancing freak."

So she truly was back to her old self. "You've had your victory, Penny. Just enjoy it and leave me alone."

"I haven't forgotten any of it. I want to make sure you know that." She wrinkled her freckled nose.

To my surprise, Ariadne spoke up. "Of course we know that. I've got a *bandage* around my head to remind me, haven't I?"

I looked at her, open-mouthed.

Penny froze for a moment, but then her mouth twisted into a grim smile. "Have fun," she said flatly.

I picked up my shoe and tried to throw it at her, but she pulled the door shut in front of her just in time.

The next ballet lesson, Penny was welcomed back. "You all know Penelope Winchester," said Miss Finch, gesturing at her. "It seems she was wrongly banned from attending class." This caused quite a commotion, and our teacher waved her hands to quiet everyone down. "Let's keep the past in the past, shall we? I hope you'll be on your best behaviour from now on, Miss Winchester."

"Yes, Miss," she replied.

Penny was true to her word, and I was able to practise in peace. It was strangely liberating and I felt that I danced my best that day. Even Nadia seemed in a better mood than usual.

When the bell rang and after everyone else had filed out, Miss Finch called me over. She was playing a soft, mournful tune on the piano, almost like a funeral march.

"Do you like this piano?" I asked, as I approached.

"Oh yes," she said. "It's not quite the same as my last one, but... it's close enough." She carried on playing. "It still sings."

I smiled at that. "You wanted to speak to me?"

"Yes. In fact, it's about this very piano. I had it tuned at the weekend, and it turned up something rather interesting."

She bent over and picked up a floral carpet bag from the floor. After rummaging inside of it, she made an 'ah' sound and pulled something out.

Paper. Oh goodness, is that what I think it is?

I made a suitably blank expression, hoping to conceal my inner turmoil.

She held the pages out. "I think these might be for you."

Gingerly, I took them and opened them up. It was Scarlet's writing for sure. But how...?

Wait. We hadn't checked the last pages for a clue, had we? After all the mayhem up on the roof it hadn't occurred to me to do so. Whatever Scarlet's clue had been, I'd missed it, and now Miss Finch had the pages. I could have kicked myself for being so stupid.

"They were hidden inside the lid. As soon as the tuning

man gave them to me, I thought of Scarlet, after what you'd told me about her smashing the old piano."

I nodded, still unsure of what to say. "Did you read them?" I dreaded to think what they said.

"At first, I thought it might have been an apology from her. But when I saw that it was a diary entry, I didn't look at it. I knew it wasn't meant for my eyes."

"Oh, thank you, Miss." I sighed with relief. "But how did you know it was by Scarlet?"

"She used to write me notes sometimes, did you know that?"

"No," I said, surprised.

"She just left me little letters about looking forward to class, asking about when I used to dance professionally, things like that." She smiled wanly. "I thought I recognised the handwriting, and if anyone would hide something in the new piano, it would be her."

I nodded and folded the pages up tightly.

"I hope one day you'll tell me what this was all about."

"I hope I'll be able to," I said, sincerely. "Thank you. You have no idea what this means to me."

I managed to make it back to the safety of the dorm without being scolded for running. This time I made sure the door was firmly shut behind me – I didn't want another Penny episode. If only it had a lock as well.

The room was chilly as usual, so I put on a cardigan over my ballet clothes and climbed under the blankets with the diary pages.

Dear Diary,

Something has just happened, something so unbelievable that I'm not sure if I can even write it down. I feel cold inside.

I trembled as I read those lines. What could I be about to read?

I really did go too far. Violet and Penny were spitting with anger and they hunted me down. I was asleep in bed when they came for me, them and their awful friends. I tried everything to fight them off, biting and kicking, but they dragged me up to the rooftop. They'd even found out about my secret place. Now nowhere here is safe.

It was freezing cold and dark, with only the light of the moon and the stars. Violet pinned me to the tiles and Penny spat in my face. I wiped my eyes and tried to scramble to my feet, and then I heard the click of a lock. At first I thought they'd gone and left me there, but it was worse – they'd left me with Violet.

She just stood there, her hair blowing about her face.

"You thought you'd get away with all of it, didn't you," she said in a voice as cold as the night.

I said nothing.

"Well, I know all about you, Scarlet Grey, I know everything about your pathetic little life. I know what you did to get into this school."

"You're lying," I said, and I went to lunge at her, but she darted sideways and I lost sight of her.

Then she reappeared, a shadow between the tall chimney stacks, pacing up and down with her hands clasped behind her back like a military commander. "You may have tried to hide the evidence in your precious diary, but I found it. And I knew exactly what to do with it. I will get you thrown out of this school for good. You never should have come here!"

"You little sneak!" I yelled. "You, you..."

She charged towards me, as if my words were bouncing off her. "I _will_ get you thrown out and I _will_ tell your twin the truth. How would that make her feel, hmm?"

I slapped her, hard, and then I tried to wrestle her to the ground. But she got the better of me, clawing at my face until I fell back and cried out...

And that was when the hatch burst open, and Miss Fox appeared.

She was screaming something at us, but I was too caught up in tackling Violet to hear her. And then Violet's weight was lifted from me as Miss Fox grabbed Violet by the ear and hauled her over to the edge of the rooftop.

"WHAT IS THE MEANING OF ALL THIS?" she screeched. I was winded, trying to get my breath back, so I couldn't say a word.

Violet twisted out of her grip. "Scarlet started it, Miss, I found out that she—"

But before she had even finished, Miss Fox had hold of her again. "You mistake me for someone who cares for your excuses," she said through gritted teeth. "You DARE to break the rules in my school? I will make you sorry you were even born, mark my words!"

And then Violet started yelling back. I couldn't believe anyone would dare to take on Miss Fox, but she did. "You'll be sorry if you lay a hand on me! I watch people, I know things."

"What are you—" snapped Miss Fox, but Violet interrupted her. "I'll tell everyone, I swear it. I'll tell them what's in your desk drawer and—"

And those were the last words I ever heard Violet speak. Miss Fox spun her around and clamped a hand over her mouth. I was lying on the tiles by the open roof hatch, and I watched as Violet's eyes silently turned from fury to pleading. They were perilously close to the roof edge.

Then, still keeping hold of Violet, Miss Fox strode over to me. I went to stand and she shoved me so hard in the stomach that I crumpled over and fell down through the hatch on to the steps below. The Fox slammed the hatch shut above me, and somehow locked it from the outside. I pushed it as hard as I could, banged my fists on it, loudly enough to wake the dead, or so I thought. Yet there was no response from the other side, and no one came running. I could see nothing but darkness out of the hatch window.

I waited there for what seemed like hours.

Now I've returned to the dorm, and I just don't know what to do. What just happened seems unreal. Like a dream.

Or a nightmare.

I realised I was holding my breath. The words washed over me and threatened to pull me under. Miss Fox had a secret. One so terrible she'd do anything to keep it hidden. This was a huge discovery, and it twisted my stomach.

I thought the pages had ended, but there was more.

Dear Diary,

Violet didn't come back that night. I went to lessons as usual, and when I returned all of her things were gone. Even her bed was pristine. It's almost as if she never existed.

I've always wanted to get rid of her, but not like this! What if... what if Miss Fox pushed her off the roof?

Penny knocked on my door and asked where Violet was,

over and over. I told her I had no idea, but she doesn't seem to believe me. "If you did something to her, I will find out what it was, and I will kill you," she said. I closed the door in her face.

So now I must confront Miss Fox. I can't let her get away with this.

If she can make Violet disappear, what might she do to me?

Chapter Twenty-Eight

I shuddered. Miss Fox was clearly determined to silence anyone who got close to her secrets.

I was awash with panic and unease as I turned over the last sheet of paper.

It simply said:

The End...

I frowned. There had to be more!

Was Scarlet being contrary? Was she trying to tell me that this wasn't quite the end? That I'd find the ending somewhere else?

I must tell Ariadne.

As if by magic, she shuffled into the room. She looked a little ropey, but happy. "I was excused from hockey," she said. "With a note from the nurse. I had to write an essay about the benefits of fresh air and exercise instead."

That seemed a pretty strange thing to be happy about, but Ariadne was strange by nature. She flopped on to her bed contentedly.

I waved the new pages at her. "Look what Miss Finch found. I can't believe it."

She sat up straight away. "Oh. My. GOSH. Is that what I think it is?"

"She found them in the piano, but she swears she didn't read them."

I didn't think I could explain everything I'd just read to Ariadne so I handed both the entries over. I watched Ariadne's eyes grow wider as she read, her lips moving along with the words.

When she had finished, she just put the pages down in front of her gently. Her face had turned the shade of our morning porridge. I imagine mine looked similar. "Miss Fox... made Violet vanish? Took her away somewhere or... worse?"

I shook my head. "How can we know? Scarlet didn't see what happened."

Ariadne's eyes lit up. "Let's look at what we do know," she said. "So neither of them came back down the hatch, but even if Miss Fox pushed Violet from the roof, she can't have jumped off herself, can she?"

"Unless she turned into a bat and flew off into the night." Reading *Dracula* had clearly had an effect on me.

"Exactly."

I thought about it for a moment and then the answer hit me. "There's another hatch! Another way off the roof!"

Ariadne flapped her arms frantically. "We have to look!"

In unison, we turned to the window and peered at the outside world. The sky was iron grey and it was blowing a gale, the trees bending at the force of the wind and the driving rain.

"Tomorrow?"

"Tomorrow."

I lay awake thinking about what we'd found out. Miss Fox was behind all of this, pulling the strings, I just knew it.

"Ivy?" Ariadne whispered to me from the other side of the room.

"Yes?"

"We're close. I can sense it."

I grinned in the dark. "You've got psychic powers now, have you?"

She threw her teddy bear at me. "No, silly. But I've got a feeling. We'll find the missing piece. These things are always in the last place you think to look, aren't they? Like the time I lost my pony."

I propped myself up on one elbow. "You lost your pony?"

"I wasn't allowed out for two days and the stable boy forgot to feed him, so Oswald kicked the gate down and trotted to the local village. I found him in the Thompsons' back garden. The Thompson boys were feeding him jelly beans..."

I started laughing quietly. "Are you saying the final bit of Scarlet's diary is going to be in someone's back garden?"

Ariadne tried to look indignant, but her expression soon cracked into a smile. "No, but the Thompsons' was the last place I thought of." Then her expression turned sad, and she pulled the sheets up higher. "Of course, that was what made Father say Oswald was too much trouble. I had to sell him."

"Oh, I'm so sorry..."

"It's all right." She sighed. "He was very naughty anyway."

"Well, hopefully when you finish school you can get another pony. Or a whole horse!"

"I wouldn't want *half* a horse," she replied.

Not long later, Ariadne was fast asleep, but images of my sister, of Miss Fox, of Violet kept flashing through my mind.

Silently, I prayed that the next day would bring clear skies so that we could investigate up on the roof.

I struggled to think what '*The End*...' could mean. Were we close to the final entries, should we think about where the story could end? Or was it literal? Perhaps the last pages would be hidden inside a book...

These thoughts dragged at me through the night, until I finally succumbed to sleep.

When I awoke the next day, I rushed to the window. The sky was the grey of old linen, with the sun nowhere in sight. But there was no rain or wind, so we were safe to go up on the roof. I shook Ariadne awake and told her the good news.

We still had to attend lessons, and I was so distracted I was probably doing a better impression of Scarlet than ever. Arithmetic was a blur and geography a nuisance. I wanted nothing more than for the bell to ring out and let the school day be over.

At lunchtime I went to the library, hopefully flicking through the endings of a few of the books I knew Scarlet had read, gaining myself some strange looks from the librarian. But wherever the end was, this wasn't it.

Three o'clock came eventually, and I hurried to meet Ariadne at the bottom of the stairwell that led up to the roof. She was already bouncing up and down when I got there.

"So much for being inconspicuous, Ariadne," I teased.

She turned around. "Oh, I— Scarlet!" Her voice lowered to a whisper. "I'm just so excited. I know it's strange, but this could be our chance to find... something. Everything! I've been thinking about it. This place was Scarlet's secret sanctuary, and what happened to Violet happened up here. What if *this* is what she meant? What if this is the end?"

I knew what she meant, but at the same time I couldn't bring myself to share her excitement. I might be about to find out how my sister had died. I wanted to know – no, I *needed* to know, for myself as well as for her sake, but the thought made me feel numb inside. Then it would be *real* and I would be more alone than ever.

Somehow, my face expressed this without saying a word. Ariadne put a kind hand on my shoulder, and together we slowly climbed the stairs. But when we came to the roof hatch, a terrible sight met our eyes.

Someone had fitted a brand-new lock – big, golden and expensive-looking. Anyone could have been responsible – the caretaker, Miss Fox, maybe even Penny, although I doubted her locksmith skills. And now our last hope was gone.

I sank down against the cold wall. Ariadne ran over to the lock, muttering, "No, no," to herself. I watched as she pulled out a pin from her hair and tried her old methods on it in vain. There was a *snap* as the hairpin broke and Ariadne cried out in frustration.

"Leave it, Ariadne," I said. "We can't get up there."

To my surprise, she started to cry. Tears trickled down her cheeks. "I'm so sorry!"

It was enough to drag me out of my stupor. "Why are you sorry? It's not your fault someone put a lock on the hatch. There's nothing we can do."

She wiped her eyes on her sleeve and sat down next to me, sniffling. "I shouldn't have said we were going to find it. I gave you –" *sniff* – "false hope. Oh, Ivy, what if we can't ever get up there? The truth could be lost forever!"

I put my arm around her and let her cry. "We could try to find the other hatch," I said, but I had little hope for that either. Struggling to our feet, we searched the top corridor. There were several doors, but they were all either firmly locked or led to dusty broom cupboards. I supposed that when Rookwood was a grand stately home, this would have been the servant's quarters.

Soon I was on the verge of tears myself. Ariadne had calmed down a little, but she looked no less upset.

"It's hopeless," she said. "Truly hopeless." A moment of silence. "Unless—"

I grabbed her arm. "Unless? There's an unless?"

You couldn't interrupt Ariadne when her brain was working. She shook her head as if to clear her thoughts, but her eyes were glazed. "It could be... it could be possible."

I shook her, gently. "Ariadne, tell me what you're thinking."

"If there's a lock, there's a key. What's to say we can't find it?"

She was right. "Yes! Oh yes..." I stared at the wall, trying to see the full picture that was building in my head. "And who keeps all the school keys in her many pockets?" I remembered that day – already seeming so long ago now – when Miss Fox had jangled up the stairs, unlocked the door of room thirteen and abandoned me with my luggage. She had pocketed the silver key and its brown paper label. "With labels on, no less! Miss Fox will have it, I'm certain."

Ariadne looked crestfallen. "But do we have *any* chance of getting it from her?"

"Maybe if we distract her. Or –" my face lit up – "we give her a reason to change her dress."

"Yes, make a tear in it, or... or... spill something on it!"

"Giving us the time to steal the key!"

We stood there in the hallway, both breathless with the flow of ideas. And I watched as, slowly, Ariadne's mousy features stretched into a wide grin. With her mane of hair haloed in the light from the window hatch, she was suddenly no longer a mouse, but a lion.

"I have a plan," she said.

Chapter Twenty-Nine

It was crazy. It was ridiculous. It was certainly going to get us into trouble. And there was the vague, tiny, miniscule chance that Ariadne's plan might just work.

The first thing we had to find was a bag of flour. My immediate thought was to get some from the storeroom in the wine cellar. But Ariadne had a less risky idea that didn't involve another night-time kitchen trip. She hid a bag of the stuff in her satchel during home economics, along with a bottle of bright red food colouring.

By dinner, I was sitting at our usual table alone. *I really hope you know what you're doing, Ariadne*, I thought.

Dinner time was the one occasion when we knew for certain where Miss Fox would be. She was always in the hall, tapping that infernal cane against her leg and staring daggers at potential wrongdoers.

I watched the clock, feeling its ticking in my bones even though I couldn't hear it over the din. When Ariadne finally walked in, clutching the bowl that contained her concoction, I almost choked on my stew.

She caught my eye and I nodded at her – imperceptibly, I hoped.

Then her look of determination melted into her familiar, half-dazed expression. She ambled in the direction of the kitchen, some of the red gloopy liquid sloshing over the side of the bowl as she moved.

Nothing escaped Miss Fox. Her eyebrows knitted and she jerked out in front of Ariadne, pockets jangling, cane whooshing at her side. "Miss Flitworth, what do you think you're—?"

And at that, Ariadne tripped. And chucked the entire mess down the front of Miss Fox's pristine black dress.

Miss Fox screamed. It was like a growl and a whine and a high-pitched roar all rolled into one.

The whole hall went silent. I could barely breathe, but

Ariadne had her role down to a T. She burst into tears. "Oh, Miss, I'm so sorry, Miss, I was trying to make a jelly but it all went wrong and I just wanted to ask the cooks what had happened and I didn't mean to spill it and..."

To my surprise, Miss Fox didn't shout at her. Nor did she immediately threaten a caning. In fact, she was turning an interesting shade of puce. *She's embarrassed*, I realised. *The Fox, embarrassed!*

The silence lingered a while longer. Then Miss Fox said, very quietly, "Go to your room, Miss Flitworth. Save your cookery for class."

"Oh, Miss, of course, anything you say, Miss," sobbed Ariadne. But Miss Fox merely held up a finger, and she shut up. All eyes were on Miss Fox, as she tried to walk from the room in a dignified manner. Her dress dripped specks of the goo on to the floor as she passed.

A few minutes later, when everyone could be sure she was out of earshot, the whole room descended into chaos. Girls were laughing and giggling and calling "did you see that?" to each other. The teachers tried frantically to calm everyone down, waving and shushing in vain.

And this was where my part came in. I stood up.

"Where are you off to, Scarlet?" asked Mrs Knight, exasperated. "You've barely touched your stew, and there's still pudding to come."

"Permission to go and see if Ariadne is all right, Miss?"

She nodded thoughtfully. "Well, I suppose that's fine. But be quick."

I snuck out into the corridor and ran in the direction of Miss Fox's office. With my ear to the door, I could hear her banging about in there. *Ariadne had better be right about her changing her dress*, I thought, *otherwise we're back to square one*.

But then I heard a louder noise nearer the door and had to fling myself out of the way as it opened. Miss Fox hurried out of her office and into the nearby door marked 'Staff Lavatories'. She was holding another black dress over her arm, one that appeared much the same as the one she always wore that was currently dripping red gloop. She must have had a whole set of them.

The main door to the lavatories had a big keyhole without a cover on it. Perfect. I tiptoed over and knelt down. Since everyone else was at dinner, there was no one around to notice my strange behaviour. I threw a few furtive glances over my shoulder, and then peered through the keyhole.

Miss Fox was leaning over the sink, scrubbing furiously at her dress. Ariadne's concoction would come out of such tough material fairly easily, but the dress really was covered in it. For a moment I feared she would just clean it off and then come back out, but then she threw her arms to the side in frustration.

She began to pull the various keys out of her pockets and pile them on to the side of the sink. There was one big bunch and a fair few smaller ones on their own, with familiar brown paper labels. As she leant over, I spotted another key that she didn't remove – one on a black velvet ribbon knotted around her neck. *Curiouser and curiouser.*

Then, satisfied that her pockets were empty, she walked into a stall to change her dress. This was my cue. I held my breath and turned the handle of the door as gently as I could. I tiptoed across the tiles. Miss Fox was only a heartbeat away.

The pile of keys on the sink – brass and copper and silver in colour – seemed endless. My eyes darted from one to the next. Where was the one I needed? I skimmed the labels in desperation: *Kitchens*, *Library*, *Basement*.

And then I saw it, almost dangling off the side: *Roof*.

I reached for it with the tips of my fingers. Rustling noises came from the stall – Miss Fox must have nearly finished changing.

The key made an almost imperceptible *glingling* noise as I picked it up, but it was like an alarm bell in my head.

Yet the stall door remained closed and, still tiptoeing, still not daring to breathe, I made my way back to the door and out into the corridor.

I'd done it. I'd got the key! I leant against the wall, my lungs desperate to make up the breaths I'd held in.

And then I was away, running for Ariadne, for the roof, for my sister.

Ariadne was waiting in our room. She jumped up, grinning when I came in. "Did you see? Oh my goodness, Ivy, the look on Miss Fox's face when I spilled that slop on her! I'd do it again any time!" A pause. "Did it work? Did you get the key?"

Slowly, I pulled up the key by its label and dangled it in front of Ariadne.

Her face turned deadly serious. "Let's go," she said.

The key fitted the lock. I turned it, and it popped open. I looked back at my friend – my best friend – her eyes were wide with fear.

I took her hand and squeezed it. "It'll be okay this time. There's no rain on the rooftop and no Penny. Just stay behind me."

Ariadne nodded, and together we climbed out on to the roof.

The sky was painted with a sunset. Pinks, oranges, purples – all these delightful colours that I'd almost forgotten in a place where everything seemed to be in black and white and hues of grey. Last wisps of cloud clung to the horizon as the sun sank behind it, its dying light rippling over the landscape.

I'd had no time to appreciate it before, in the rain and the horror of Penny stealing the diary. The fields were like a picnic blanket spread over the world, all greens and yellows in the evening light; the village and the church and the shimmering lake nestling amongst them. You could see people down there, tiny silhouettes, finishing their last jobs of the day.

"This is it," I said. I somehow felt sure that Ariadne was right. This was Scarlet's place. She was in the air and the birds and the sky all around.

Ariadne said nothing. She was staring at the sunset, her mouth hanging a little open. Sometimes I forgot that she was just as much of a prisoner in this place as I was. But there wasn't time to appreciate our rooftop freedom. We had a diary entry to find.

I took my friend's hand again and helped her over the tiles. We walked along the flat of the roof, scouring it for anything that looked like a hiding place.

"Over there!" said Ariadne suddenly, pointing. Just over an arch in the roof (around eye level) was another flat area, and there was a square of wooden planks set into the tiles.

A trapdoor?

"It has to be how Miss Fox got away that night," I said. "Let's climb over and take a look." Ariadne winced. "Okay, then," I corrected, "*I'll* climb over and take a look."

I scrambled up the tiles fairly easily, though I laddered my stockings on one of the sharp edges. Once at the top, I slid down the other side. It certainly wasn't out of the question for Miss Fox to escape that way with or without Violet – after all, she was taller and stronger than me. I shivered a little, despite myself. It was unusually warm and sunny for an evening, but a chill breeze was on the air. Goose bumps prickled at my arms as I made for the trapdoor.

Unsurprisingly, it was locked. It had an iron ring, which I pulled on with all my might, but it didn't give.

"Try jumping on it!" shouted Ariadne from the other side of the roof. I gave her a look. The last thing I needed was to go crashing through the ceiling.

And after all, it was the diary I needed to find. "If Scarlet left the pages up here, they need to be inside something. Like a container or a pot."

Ariadne looked around. "A chimney pot?"

I started to laugh, but then it dawned on me. Ariadne was serious. Scarlet really could have hidden them in a chimney pot, if that chimney no longer led to a fire...

By the time I'd climbed back over to her, she'd already

pulled a map of the school from her dress. "This one," she said, pointing over at one of the chimney stacks. "It's above the baths and some of the classrooms. I shouldn't think there's been a fire underneath it for quite some years."

Looking down at her map, I followed her fingers as she traced out what she meant. "You're right, Ariadne! You're right!" I almost picked her up and span her around, but I had a feeling that wasn't advisable for a person who'd recently suffered from concussion.

I scrambled over to the chimney. This could *really* be it.

The pots on the stack were old, with crown-shaped tops. I stood on tiptoe and reached into the nearest one, the clay scratching my skin... Nothing. I turned back and looked at Ariadne, who smiled reassuringly.

My hand shook as I tried the next chimney pot, but that too seemed empty. I began to panic. What if we'd been wrong? What if this wasn't the final hiding place? What if...

And then I felt something. Not pages, but an object, cold and metal.

I managed to get my fingers around it and pull it out. It was a small box tied with an elastic band, and the words 'THE END' crudely scratched into the lid.

"Oh, Scarlet," I whispered.

I carried the box back to Ariadne, holding it out reverently.

She stared at it. "Shall we... shall we open it?"

Ariadne and I sat down on the tiles, and looked out over the fields as the fiery glow of the sunset fell away and the world turned to black.

It was time to find out how my sister died.

Chapter Thirty

That little box was everything to me; the reason I was here and the reason I hadn't run for my life as soon as I'd arrived at this awful place. All of my hopes and fears were riding on it.

I pinged off the rubber band holding it closed and opened the lid. It was stuffed with folded pages, flowing with writing.

We'd found it.

Tears came to my eyes. "Oh, Ariadne," I said, "should I read this? I mean, Scarlet's death, I don't know if I can…"

My best friend put a gentle hand on my shoulder. "Ivy Grey, if you don't open that box right now, I will throw you off the roof myself." She grinned.

I unfolded the pages and flattened them out against my skirt. In the fading light, Ariadne and I began to read, together.

Dear Diary,

Violet never came back. Miss Fox called an assembly and casually mentioned in the notices that Violet's guardian, a lawyer named Mister Roberts, had whisked her abroad to attend an exclusive academy in France. I sat there open-mouthed. I glanced around at everyone else – couldn't they tell she was lying? To the whole school, no less?

Penny was the only one who didn't look as though she believed it either. When our eyes met, she stared at me furiously until I had to look away. She's convinced that I had something to do with it. And why wouldn't she be? As far as she knows, I was the last person to see Violet.

Later, in the hallway, Penny took me by the collar and started screaming at me, demanding answers. It was cowardly, I know, but I didn't tell her. Partly because I was scared of what Miss Fox would do to me, and partly because Penny still thought she could treat me like dirt. I stamped on her foot and twisted away from her.

To my surprise, she started to cry. Proper, ugly crying.

I thought I'd hurt her, but I soon realised – she was truly upset. She couldn't understand why Violet had abandoned her.

Then that new girl came over, the one from India, Nadia Sayani. She put her arm around Penny and glared at me, started whispering to her. "You leave her alone," she said to me, fiercely. "I don't know what you've done, but I'll find out." Then she marched Penny away, still sobbing.

I tried to go back to the roof, but I couldn't bear it. To my surprise, the hatch was open again. It was like none of it had even happened.

So there's no other choice. I have to confront Miss Fox. I already know too much, and I'm certain that it's only a matter of time before she finds a way to get rid of me too. Perhaps I can threaten her with what I saw, what I heard...

Besides all that, something deep inside tells me that it's the right thing to do. Maybe I should stay away and save myself. But what would Ivy do? She would get to the truth. She would try to help Violet, no matter how much of an awful person Violet was.

I hope Miss Fox is ready for me.

Ariadne and I shared a fearful glance.

Dear Diary,

I feared the worst, but this... this is something else. I'm not sure how much time I have.

I walked into Miss Fox's office like a criminal going to the gallows. I wondered if she'd throw me out, but she just shut the door and demanded to know what I wanted.

Well, I gave it my best shot. I pretended I knew what Violet had been getting at. "You can't keep your secrets locked up forever!" I yelled at her. "You can't just make your problems disappear! Why don't you show me what's in your drawer?" Her eyes flickered to the top one, just for a moment, and I knew Violet was right. "Yes, that one," I said, pointing.

Her expression became blank. "I can make things very unpleasant for you, Scarlet Grey," she said.

I swallowed.

"I think perhaps your mind doesn't work properly. Perhaps you need to see a doctor."

"I saw what you did to Violet, Miss," I snarled. "I saw you take her, maybe you even killed her. You won't get away with it, and you won't convince me that I didn't see what I saw."

She grabbed me by the front of my dress. I tried to back away, but she had an iron grip. "Oh, do you really think so?" she said, and I had never heard her sound so nasty. My stomach lurched and I felt my body contract with fear. "You... you can't hurt me," was all I could say.

She smiled, and it was the most unpleasant thing I had ever

seen. "If you think I can't, then you have grossly underestimated me."

I went to push her, and I think I caught her off guard, but as I ran to the door I tripped on her cane. My ankle twisted as I slammed into the ground, and a sharp pain ripped through it.

Miss Fox stood over me. "I'm giving you an ultimatum, Miss Grey. I don't want a single soul to hear of this. If you leave, go somewhere far away and never mention Rookwood again, we can forget about this matter."

I blinked up at her, disbelieving. "I can't leave. Everyone will want to know where I've gone! What about school? What about my father? You can't just replace me!"

At this point she sat down in her chair, and after a long pause she pulled out a file from her desk and rifled through it. "You have a twin, I see. Didn't quite get the best marks in the entrance exam. It seems that you may, in fact, be easily replaceable."

Replaceable. She wants to replace me. With Ivy.

I tried to edge away, the pain shooting from my ankle. I'll run away, I told myself. I'll just run from the school as soon as she lets me out of here, and I'll find someone and get them to tell the police.

Miss Fox's eyes flicked up at me then, as if she had plucked my thoughts straight out of my head. "If you're thinking of running away, Miss Grey, I assure you, you will not get far. I have people watching the gates and patrolling the grounds for students that cannot follow the rules. I have teachers who will do whatever I tell them."

Was she bluffing? I couldn't tell.

Miss Fox had won.

I'm in my room now, alone, gazing at the side of the room with the empty bed and the bare cupboard.

One thing is certain. I need Ivy to know what's happened. I need the world to know I existed, in case Miss Fox makes me disappear, just like Violet.

I don't want to be lost forever.

The final two pages were different. Different paper. It was another letter, addressed to me with the words 'The Beginning' at the top of the page. I looked at Ariadne, and she averted her eyes.

Dearest Ivy, you are my only hope.

We've always been together, and I know I've never really done anything for you, but now I must rely on you completely.

I'm going to hide my diary pages in secret places so that hopefully you will be the only one to find it. Just like when we were little. And if anyone else finds a piece, I pray that they won't understand what it is they've found. Otherwise everything will be lost.

Someone has to know the truth. The whole truth. About me, and Violet.

And speaking of truth – Ivy, I'm so sorry. I switched our entrance exam papers. I saw the chance to be better and I took it. So I'm responsible for this whole mess. All of it.

I just hope that one day you can find it in your heart to forgive me. If anyone can solve this, you can.

Your twin,

Scarlet

I thought I would cry. I thought I would cry until my eyes were empty.

Oh, Scarlet, of course I forgive you. She had more than paid for her mistake. I would forgive her everything and more, just to have her back again.

Unexpectedly, I then began to feel strangely calm. This wasn't the serene calm of lazy Sundays at Aunt Phoebe's. This was the calm before the storm.

Miss Fox thought she could take my sister away from me? She thought she could control everything and replace anyone who got in the way? I stood up, fists clenched. It was getting cold up there on the roof as it grew dark, but I wasn't shivering any longer.

"Ariadne," I said, my voice level. "I know what we have to do."

Chapter Thirty-One

I hurried down from the roof, the little metal box clutched in my hands. "Think about it, Ariadne. What was the mistake that Scarlet made?"

Ariadne trotted after me. "I don't know, what?"

"She went alone." That was Scarlet, always wanting to do things by herself. "She didn't tell anyone that she was going to confront the Fox. She only wrote it in her diary."

"Because she didn't trust anyone! She..." I turned back to Ariadne.

"She only trusted you," she finished.

I bit my lip, and nodded. We carried on down the corridor until we got to our dorm room. Dinner had finished, and giggles about the incident with Miss Fox and Ariadne's concoction were still spreading. A couple of girls pointed and laughed as they caught sight of us. Ariadne, in an unexpected gesture, bowed at them, and they gave her a round of applause.

As we darted into room thirteen, I pulled the pages out of the box. "I have to finish what Scarlet started. I have to face Miss Fox, but I won't be alone. I'll have you."

I looked up at Ariadne, expectantly. She grinned. "Always."

I couldn't help but smile, then. Nothing could make up for losing a twin, but gaining such a friend as Ariadne had made a real difference to me.

Crouching down by my bed, I stuffed the little box into the mattress with the rest of the diary. I'd kept the final pages, the letter from Scarlet, tucked inside my waistband.

"What are you doing?" asked Ariadne. "Don't we need to show that to Miss Fox? To get her to confess?"

I brushed my hands off on my skirt as I stood up. "No, it's too risky. If she gets her hands on the box and the diary then there'd be no proof that any of this ever happened. And −" I stared down at my mattress − "there's someone who already knows about the diary and where I hide it, someone who *owes* us..."

Ariadne raised her eyebrows, making her look like a puzzled owl.

"Are you ready for this?" I asked.

"Ready as I'll ever be." She took a deep breath. "If we end up dead, promise me we'll haunt Miss Fox together?"

"I promise. Rattling chains and all."

I knocked on the door to Penny's room, and Nadia opened it. She looked uncharacteristically cheery.

"Scarlet," she said. "I wanted to thank you."

I almost fell over backwards. "Why?"

"For that," she replied, opening the door a little wider and gesturing at the bed. Penny was lying there fast asleep, snoring contentedly. "I don't know what you did, but she's like a different person. She told me it was because of *you* that she was allowed to dance again."

Nadia turned to Ariadne. "And you... Scarlet's friend. What you did earlier was hilarious. I don't know if it was on purpose or not, but I've never laughed so much."

In this mood I hoped that Nadia might be open to doing what I was about to ask of her. "Nadia, listen. We have a favour to ask."

She nodded. "Mmm, go on."

"After lights out, can you knock on our door? If we're not there I need you to wake Penny. Tell her that... tell her it's about what she found, that there's more of it. She knows where to look. Tell her we've gone to make things right."

Nadia's eyebrows knitted. "All right," she said, after a pause. "And she'll know what this means?"

"Yes. If we're back, don't worry about it. We can tell her ourselves."

"Fine," she said, then she gave a parting grin and pulled the door shut.

"What was that about?" asked Ariadne.

"Insurance policy," I replied. "If we don't come back, Nadia will pass on that message and Penny will read the diary. She'll know what's happened."

Ariadne's mouth dropped open. "Brilliant," she whispered.

I couldn't believe what we were about to do. The corridor seemed endless, and when we got to the stairs I felt like every step sent a shock through my body.

Halfway down, Ariadne grabbed hold of my arm and gripped so tightly that her knuckles turned white. "This is really happening, isn't it?" she said under her breath.

I placed my hand over hers. "It might be a nightmare, you know. I'm not sure yet."

We reached the bottom floor and headed along the corridor. Mrs Knight spotted us and shouted something, but I paid no heed to her. She was merely a small fish; Miss Fox was the shark.

The office door loomed ahead of us, and I felt my fear grow at the thought of going in there, of what might happen, of those lifeless dogs staring down at us from the walls.

I knocked. I held my breath.

The door opened. "Yes?" said Miss Fox.

I stared up at her. "We need to talk to you," I said.

She looked affronted. "Where are your manners, Miss Grey?"

"Probably in the same place where you left yours." I marched into her office, leaving her open-mouthed in the doorway. Ariadne trailed behind me. She was gazing with horror at a stuffed pug dog wearing a miniature saddle.

I'm not entirely sure what came over me, but I knew I could take advantage of the Fox's confusion. I grabbed the cane from by her side and sat down in her chair.

"What on *earth* do you think you're doing?" she demanded, slamming the office door behind her.

Ariadne stood behind me, arms folded. This wasn't the same mousy girl I had once met, that was for sure.

"I'm making some changes," I said, putting the cane down behind me. "We don't think you should be in charge here any longer."

The white of Miss Fox's face began to burn an angry red. "Scarlet Grey, get out of that chair this instant, or I will—"

"Or you'll what?" I demanded. "Get rid of me like you did my sister and Violet Adams? And besides, my name is IVY."

"What are you talking about?" she said flatly.

"Let's start with what we know, shall we?" I kept talking, knowing that if I stopped I would never be able to carry on. "We know that you were so keen to hide your secrets that you got rid of Violet. Then when my sister wouldn't keep quiet, you had to get rid of her too. Because you couldn't let anyone find out about what you keep hidden in *that drawer*." I shot out my trembling hand and pointed directly at the locked top drawer of her desk.

Ariadne breathed in sharply behind me.

Miss Fox shook her head. "You don't know what you're messing with," she said.

"Oh, I think I do," I replied, sounding just like Scarlet. "I think we're messing with someone who is *very* afraid. You're terrified that people will find out that you're not completely in control."

She snorted, but I could tell I'd hit the mark. "I will not stand here and listen to children—"

Ariadne slammed her hands down on the back of the chair, making me jump. "WHAT'S IN THE DRAWER, MISS?"

Miss Fox's eyes were wide with rage. "Get out," she screeched. "I won't tell you again."

And I saw a glint around her neck. *An opportunity.*

I darted towards her and snatched the velvet ribbon from around her neck, the key to the drawer dangling on the end of it. I tossed it to Ariadne.

"Why don't we see what's in there for ourselves, Miss? What will we find?"

Miss Fox clenched her teeth, about to scream at me just as the office door opened, someone was speaking as they pushed it wide:

"Mother, this is ridiculous. I will not keep up this charade any longer..."

It was Miss Finch.

Chapter Thirty-Two

*N*o, it couldn't be true.

When Miss Finch saw me standing there, gaping, she clamped her hand over her mouth and staggered back against the door.

I had to break the silence. "She's your *mother*?"

My ballet teacher looked at me, tears shining in her eyes.

"Are you in league with her?" I demanded. "I trusted you!"

"No, Ivy, please… it's not like that," she said. She reached out to me. "She's... We're..."

Miss Fox was giving her a look that could kill, hands clenched into trembling fists. "Don't say another word, Rebecca," she said through gritted teeth. "You just couldn't keep your mouth shut, could you?"

I stared from one of them to the other. "Please tell me this isn't true. Tell me you didn't tell her about—"

But they were both ignoring me now.

Miss Finch began pleading: "I had no idea that anyone else was in here. I just wanted to tell you that I thought it was time to be open about this."

Somewhere behind me, there was the click of a desk drawer being unlocked.

Oblivious to anyone else in the room, Miss Fox had stepped towards Miss Finch, furious. "There will *never* be a time to be open about this. I told you it was to remain strictly confidential or there would be consequences, did I not?"

"I can't hide who I am forever."

"You can and you will do as I say!"

Although I felt racked with despair, I knew had to keep them distracted. "Miss Finch, how is this possible? Why are you working here?"

She blinked at me. "I don't have a choice," she said. "I have nowhere else to go."

"Silence! SILENCE!" yelled Miss Fox. She leapt forward,

snatched up her cane and brandished it like a weapon. It looked as though she would snap it in half if she gripped any tighter. "Both of you stop this, immediately." Miss Fox turned to me, the cane shivering in her hands. "Insolent child. I should have known you'd be as much trouble as your sister. You'll never find her!"

My blood felt red hot, like a fire was burning inside of me, and I felt a far cry from little Ivy who never asked questions. "What did you do to her? If you laid a finger on her, I swear I'll kill you!"

I was all set to launch myself at her when Ariadne cleared her throat, loudly.

We all turned to look at her.

She was holding two things. One was an open file brimming with papers, the other a glass keepsake box. She put the box down and held out the file, flipping through it. "Miss Fox," she said, "I'm an accountant's daughter. Things like this don't get hidden in a locked drawer for no reason. Have you been fiddling the numbers? Embezzling?"

"PUT THAT DOWN!" cried Miss Fox. "That is not—"

Ariadne ignored her. "Big transactions, like this?" She pointed at a few places on a column. "Looks like it could be bribery money to me."

I was sure that was just a stab in the dark, but Miss Fox went red and started yelling something. And then Miss Finch was yelling too and I tried to shout over them and Ariadne was waving the file and...

The telephone rang.

Everyone froze. The shrill ring pierced into me and without thinking I leant over and picked up the receiver. "Hello?"

"Hullo?" a gruff male voice crackled down the line. "Guinevere? Is that you?"

I frowned. Miss Fox's name was *Guinevere*? "I'm a student. Who is this?"

"Edgar..." The man seemed to have a violent coughing fit, and I held the telephone away from my ear until it had stopped. "Edgar Bartholomew. I'm the headmaster. Would you kindly tell me what on earth is going on, and why you're answering Miss Fox's telephone?"

I seized the opportunity. "Miss Fox is a little indisposed," I said, "on account of her attacking students and embezzling funds from the school and—"

"HOW DARE YOU?" Miss Fox swung the cane at me, but I was ready. I ducked, and instead of hitting me the hissing cane knocked a line of dog photographs off the wall, sending them spilling down on to the desk. I jumped up, my heart racing, but kept hold of the telephone.

"WHAT?" Headmaster Bartholomew roared. "Is this some kind of prank? Put Miss Fox on immediately!"

"It's for *you*, Miss," I said, holding the receiver out to her. She snatched it up immediately.

"I need to sit down," said Miss Finch. She pulled up a chair in the corner and lowered herself into it, trembling. I looked over at Ariadne – she was still standing with the file, a strange mixture of terror and excitement on her face.

I could hear shouting coming from the end of the telephone. Miss Fox was protesting. "No, sir, I most certainly did not... She isn't... No... Don't..."

The colour drained from her face.

"You can't..."

And before I knew what was happening, Miss Fox shoved me and I fell sideways, crashing into Ariadne. Both of us went sprawling to the ground, narrowly missing a stuffed Jack Russell.

Miss Fox barrelled past Miss Finch, flung open the door and ran.

Chapter Thirty-Three

The telephone swung silently over the edge of the desk, back and forth.

I scrambled up from the floor and ran to the doorway, just in time to see Miss Fox's black dress swoop around a corner. I chased after her, running faster than I'd ever thought I could, but it was no use.

It was as though she'd disappeared into thin air. I frantically searched the rooms nearby and then headed for the entrance hall. I opened one of the huge front doors and peered out, but it was dark and I could see very little. I ran down the steps, looking out over Rookwood's long drive.

Nothing. Miss Fox was gone.

When I got back to her office, it was a state. The chair was tipped over, her desk covered with the fallen photographs, drawers open and spilling their contents. And in the middle of it all sat Miss Finch, being comforted by Ariadne.

"I couldn't catch her," I said, shaking my head. "She got away." I felt so disappointed.

Ariadne came over and put her arm around me. "It's all right. She may be gone, but she won't be getting out of this one easily." She gestured at the file lying open on the desk. "I think that alone is enough to get her arrested."

"If they catch her," I said with a sigh.

Miss Finch nodded. "Well, she's not going to be setting foot in this school again, Ivy. I spoke to Mr Bartholomew after you ran out, and I told him about the files we found and that Mother – Miss Fox – had run away. He sounded positively furious. I know he's been recuperating from a long illness, but given what has happened, well, he'll have to travel back here to try and sort everything out. Mrs Knight is to be in charge in the meantime."

I picked up Miss Fox's chair from the floor and sat in it, my head in my hands. How would I ever find out the truth about Scarlet's death now?

Ariadne knelt on the floor beside me, but her attention was on Miss Finch. "Miss, how can it be true that you're Miss Fox's daughter? You couldn't be more different..."

Miss Finch sighed. She looked so tired. "The beginning is the best place to start, I suppose." She settled into her seat and began. "I was adopted as a baby. I had a happy childhood with my parents in London. Ballet was my first love. I trained from a young age, and it became my profession. I danced all over the world, and then..." She stopped, and gazed at the floor. "I had the accident, on stage one night in Russia. My leg was very badly broken. The doctor said I would walk again, but my career was over. When I was healed well enough, I travelled back home. But the news hadn't reached me. My father had suffered a heart attack. And it wasn't long before my mother passed away as well.

"I had no other family, no one else to turn to. My money ran out. So I started investigating – I hoped that if I found my birth mother, she might be willing to help me..."

"And you found Miss Fox," Ariadne finished.

Of all the people to come to for help, Miss Finch had the misfortune to seek out someone who lived for cruelty and control of others.

"Yes," agreed Miss Finch, sadly. "It turned out that she'd got pregnant very young, unmarried, and been sent to an asylum. I found out that she was a teacher, and I came here to meet with her, to ask if there was anything she could do for me. She tried to deny it completely at first, but I had proof, my birth certificate."

"I'm surprised she wanted to help you," said Ariadne.

Miss Finch frowned, and dragged her fingers through her red-tinged hair. "I'm not entirely sure if she did. But she's just so proud and so *stubborn*. If anyone found out, she thought no one would ever respect her again. She wanted to get control of me, I think, to stop me from telling anyone who I really was. So she gave me the job, and let me stay at the school, but with conditions. I couldn't tell a soul that she was my mother. It was hardly ideal, but I was desperate." My ballet teacher's eyes filled with tears. "And to think, all I wanted was to find her..."

Find her.

Miss Fox had said it.

She'd said, *"You'll never find her."*

Oh my goodness.

What if? No, I didn't dare to hope. But I had to ask.

"Miss Finch," I interrupted. "Is my sister... is Scarlet alive?"

Chapter Thirty-Four

Miss Finch leant forward and didn't say anything for a moment.

"Ivy, I'm sorry... I tried to ask my mother about it. All I got were bruises for my troubles, and she threatened to throw me out on to the street if I asked any more 'inappropriate questions'. I wish I could tell you the answer."

I hugged my knees to my chest, feeling crushed.

"Miss Fox did *something* to her, Miss, we just don't know what." said Ariadne. "Are you certain you can't think of anything that would help us?"

Miss Finch shook her head. "I really don't know. Unless… unless there's anything in *that* which could tell us." She waved a hand at the objects on the desk, the incriminating file and the glass box.

Wait a minute! We hadn't even looked in the glass box yet. I gasped and reached for it. Ariadne stood up and looked over my shoulder. I undid the catch and prised open the lid, peering into it.

There was a tiny lock of hair, reddish coloured and attached to a card monogrammed with an 'R'. I held it out to Miss Finch. "This is yours, I think." She took it and gave me a weak smile.

But there was something else. A folded piece of paper. No – a photograph.

It was of a girl, and by the scowl painted on her black and white features I could tell it was a young Miss Fox. She was standing by a pram with a big hood and wheels like a bicycle. That contained Rebecca, I supposed. But what was more interesting was the background – huge iron gates, high walls and a sign.

The sign read 'Rosemoor Asylum for Young Females'.

My mind raced.

Miss Fox made girls disappear. *Violet*. *Scarlet*. Perhaps others. Maybe she killed them. Maybe she hid them in the cellar and threw away the key.

Or maybe, just maybe, she had them locked up in an asylum.

"She might have taken Scarlet there," I whispered. Then, louder, to Ariadne and Miss Finch: "She might have taken Scarlet to the asylum!" I held up the picture and tapped the sign. "We have to go and look! Please, Miss!"

Ariadne gasped. "Of course…"

Miss Finch took the photograph from me and held it with quivering hands. "Goodness," she said. "Ivy, you could be right."

Where I had been numb, suddenly there was fire. The room came alive around me and I realised what it was – hope.

My hope had returned.

I jumped up. "Please, if there's any chance that Scarlet's there, I have to go, Miss. I have to get her out."

Miss Finch pushed herself up from the arm of the chair and got to her feet. She took a deep breath. "First things first – I have to call the police about my mother."

"Please," I whispered.

Miss Finch took my hands. "Ivy," she said. "You've been so brave, but I really need to sort out some of this mess first. The police will want to talk to me, perhaps to you as well. I promise you, we'll go tomorrow. I'll look up the address in my book, I'll find Miss Fox's driver if he's still around, and we'll get him to take us to the station. Can you be brave for one more night?"

I bit my lip so hard that it started to bleed. Tomorrow, if Scarlet was alive, I would find her.

"Yes, Miss," I said.

It was late when Ariadne and I arrived back at the dorm. To my surprise, our room was occupied.

Penny and Nadia were sitting on my bed, and they had Scarlet's diary.

"What... what are you doing here?" I asked, rubbing my bleary eyes. I heard Ariadne inhale sharply as she came in the door behind me.

"You didn't come back," said Nadia. "So I told Penny what you asked me to say. And we've just been reading this." She waved the diary at me. "Is this all true?"

I nodded, cautiously. Neither of them looked angry or threatening. In fact, Penny had red-rimmed eyes and tear-stained cheeks.

"So it was Miss Fox all along," she said, her voice unusually quiet. "Do you know what happened to Violet?" A pause. "Or your sister?"

"No, but... we think Miss Fox might have taken one or both of them to an asylum. I'm going there tomorrow." I realised there was an important detail that they were missing out on. "Oh, and, um, she might get arrested. She's run away and the police are after her."

"What?" exclaimed Nadia. "Are you serious?"

"*Deadly* serious," said Ariadne, her eyes wide.

"But it's not over," Penny whispered. "Not until we find them."

I felt my hatred for Penny beginning to fade away. I was just a girl who'd lost a twin, and she was just a girl who'd lost a friend.

I sat down next to Penny and Nadia on my bed, while Ariadne went and perched on hers. "If they're alive, we'll find them," I said. "I promise."

Penny handed me back the diary, and I cradled it in my hands, tracing the cracked leather and the scored letters. This was where it had all begun, and now I just prayed that we would have the ending I wanted.

"What are we going to do now?" asked Nadia, as Penny sniffled and wiped her eyes.

"I don't know," I said.

"I have an idea," said Ariadne, sheepishly. She got down under her bed and pulled out a box. When she opened it, it was full of sweets.

"Ariadne!" I exclaimed. "Where did you get those?"

My friend just grinned. "Nearly-midnight feast, anyone?" she said.

And that was how Ariadne and I ended up eating pear drops and fudge with our one-time enemies until we felt sick. And one sweet moment at a time, life got a little bit better.

Chapter Thirty-Five

The wind blew through the train station, scattering hats and newspapers and fallen leaves alike as it danced around us. I clung to my bag and my dress; Miss Finch grabbed a column to steady herself and hummed quietly.

The train was already waiting on the platform, the air heavy with steam. As the strong breeze pushed past us, the sun remained defiant and the sky was bright. We climbed the steps to the carriage and went to find our seats.

This was it. This was the day I would find out about

my sister.

We sat down on plush red seats, either side of the window, and I hefted my bag up on to the luggage rack. Miss Finch tugged on the window and it fell down with a *clunk*. I leant my head out and saw the station guard blowing his whistle and waving the train on.

As we pulled off from the station, and the autumn countryside began rolling by, I sat back and lost myself in thought.

Mrs Knight had let me call Aunt Phoebe on the telephone – or more accurately, call Aunt Phoebe's neighbour, Mr Phillips, as she didn't have one herself. He ran over to get her while I sat twisting the cord around my fingers.

She seemed completely puzzled as to why I was calling her. Not wanting to trouble her too much, I simply explained that, incredibly, there was a chance that Scarlet was still alive. Then, so relieved at finally being able to speak to my aunt, I told her that my first term at Rookwood School hadn't been a particularly happy one.

My aunt chastised herself for not coming to visit me, but she said she'd thought I was fine since I'd written her such a lovely letter. *Sigh*.

Then I gently explained that a teacher had been found guilty of criminal activity and that Scarlet might have been a victim but that I was going to find out for sure today.

Aunt Phoebe gasped and then after a pause unexpectedly said, "That's my Ivy. You'll find out what's happened, I'm sure of it. You're a little fighter, deep down."

I'd tried to telephone Father as well, but there was no answer. I wasn't surprised. Father was like a wall of silence, and I often wondered if I'd ever break through.

Since Miss Finch had very little money, she could only pay for my train ticket. Penny had begged us to ask about Violet too, and I promised her that we would.

I'd thanked Ariadne for everything, and I'd never seen anyone beam so much.

"You'll be back soon enough," she said. "And you know I'll always be your friend, whether there's one or two of you."

Then it was my turn to beam.

"Tickets, please." The inspector had appeared in our compartment. "Where are you off to today then, ladies?"

"We're looking for my lost twin," I replied, as Miss Finch handed him our tickets.

"Well, ma'am, I hope you find her then," he said, tipping his hat to me.

"I hope so too."

The train gave a shrill whistle as it dove into a tunnel, and everything went black.

*

Rosemoor Asylum for Young Females.

The words printed on the sign in the photograph had burned into my brain, and now I was facing them. Someone at a later date had added a smaller wooden sign below that read *Mental Hospital*.

I stood in front of the tall iron gates, hands on my hips.

"Are you ready?" asked Miss Finch.

I took a deep breath, as if the air would fill me with courage. "Let's go," I said.

The asylum was surrounded by an eerie quietness. It was a tall, bricked Victorian building with high windows, some with bars on.

We had to ring a bell to get the attention of the gatekeeper, a middle-aged man who leant out of a window and beckoned us nearer. "Visiting a relative, ladies?"

"Yes," called Miss Finch. "Well, we hope so."

As he emerged from the gatehouse to let us in, he exclaimed to Miss Finch, "Ma'am, don't I know you? Roberta, is it?"

"Rebecca." Miss Finch's eyes crinkled at the corners. "I came here some time ago, when I was tracking down my mother."

"I remember!" said the man. "Did you find her?"

"Yes," replied Miss Finch. "Unfortunately."

He grimaced. "I won't ask about that one. Please follow

the path." He waved towards the front entrance of the asylum and wandered back to his gatehouse.

My body wanted to turn and run, but my mind told me it was now or never. Whether the truth was good or bad; it was my truth, and it was Scarlet's truth. I had to find out.

The reception was small, with clinical green walls and that strange hospital smell. Miss Finch and I approached the front desk. There was a woman there, her blonde hair cut into a tight bob. She was furiously typing and sipping at a mug of coffee every few seconds.

"Excuse me," said Miss Finch, leaning on the counter.

The receptionist completely ignored her.

Miss Finch raised her eyebrows and I shrugged. She tried again, a little louder. "Excuse me!"

Still the woman didn't look up. "Welcometo-RosemoorhowcanIhelp?" she said, flatly.

"Um," said Miss Finch. "We're looking for someone who might be a patient here, a relative. They might have been incarcerated under false pretences."

"Name?"

"Scarlet Grey," I said. "Or maybe Violet Adams."

Chink. The receptionist put down her coffee mug and pulled out a large book. She opened it at the Gs, and slammed it down on the desk. She traced a finger down column after column, and I felt cold fear rising in my heart. *She's not finding anything.* I gripped the edges of the counter with nervous fingers. Then she flipped to the As and did the same.

"No one of those names here," she said. "Sorry."

I sagged. The room span. I thought I was going to throw up.

All this way for nothing. All of *this* for nothing. We must have been wrong, and Scarlet was dead, and I was alone.

"No!" I cried, the word leaping from my mouth. "No, no, please, she has to be here..."

There was a squawk and a splash – the receptionist had spilled coffee right down the front of her cardigan. But she wasn't making any effort to clean it up. She didn't appear to have even noticed it.

Because she was looking at my face like she'd seen a ghost.

"You," she said, pointing at me with a long quivering fingernail. "You're..."

Miss Finch looked just as bewildered as I felt.

The receptionist pulled herself together. "You're a twin, aren't you?"

I nodded, my eyes clouding with tears.

"Come with me," she said, as she stood up, unhooked a section of the counter and lifted it up to let herself out. Then she quickly motioned at me to follow her.

My legs carried me through a green door and out into a corridor. I heard the soft tread of Miss Finch's shoes as she followed behind me. I felt light-headed and hardly dared to guess what was happening.

The corridor led to a door and, once unlocked, the door led to the outside. The woman swiftly led us up a stone path and around the back of the building. "It's faster this way," she said, not looking around.

"You go on ahead," panted Miss Finch. I turned, and saw that she was leaning heavily on her good leg. "I'll catch you up."

The receptionist strode on ahead, disappearing around a corner.

"Are you sure?" I asked.

"I'll be all right in a minute," said Miss Finch. "And you will be fine. You always are."

I don't know why, but I curtseyed. I'm not sure if it was nerves, or something else, but Miss Finch smiled encouragingly. "Go on," she said.

I continued down the path. At the very back of the building, there was a courtyard. The sun spilled into it, illuminating box hedges and dying roses and autumn leaves, glinting off the water of a fountain at the centre. The fountain sat in a raised square pond, shallow and bare. But as I looked into it, I saw a flash of orange – a goldfish. Scarlet's favourite.

The back of the asylum featured enormous floor-to-ceiling windows with French doors in the centre, and I supposed this was where the receptionist had gone.

As I headed for the doors, something stopped me dead in my tracks.

My reflection.

There it was, in the window. The same long dark hair, the same pale skin, the same tiny birthmark.

I stepped forward, and the reflection stepped forward. I held up my hand...

And the reflection didn't move.

It stared at me.

She stared at me.

And then Scarlet's hand moved too, and met mine against the cool glass.

This is the story of how I found my sister.

Acknowledgements

There are so many people that I would like to extend my thanks to that I cannot possibly fit them all in here. But I hope that if they all squish up a bit, there will be room for as many as possible. So without further ado, my thanks go to:

My wonderful editors, Lizzie Clifford and Lauren Buckland, and the team at HarperCollins for their hard work towards putting this book into your hands. My equally wonderful and brave agent Jenny Savill for taking a chance on me and my writing, and all at the Andrew Nurnberg Associates. The lovely creative writing students and teachers at Bath Spa University, particularly those on the MA Writing For Young People led by Julia Green – you made this possible, and you were excellent beta readers! A special mention to Janine Amos, whose lesson brought Scarlet and Ivy to life.

There are others who have helped this book on its journey in some way or another, providing love and support, or just being there to prevent writing-related meltdowns. To name but a few: my family and family-in-law, Ed, the Bousfields, Charlie, Dominic, Erin, Sarah, and all the local gang. Thanks also to those who follow me in cyberspace, and the gang at r/YA Writers who are always on hand with useful advice. And for providing limitless inspiration, I am forever indebted to Terry, Neil and Tuomas.

Finally, thank you for reading. Rookwood School will be keeping its doors open...

OUT NOW

Rookwood School at midnight is a scary place to be…

SCARLET
and
IVY

The Whispers in the Walls

SOPHIE CLEVERLY

The wind is howling.
The rain is freezing.
But that's not the reason why pupils at Rookwood School
are feeling the chill …

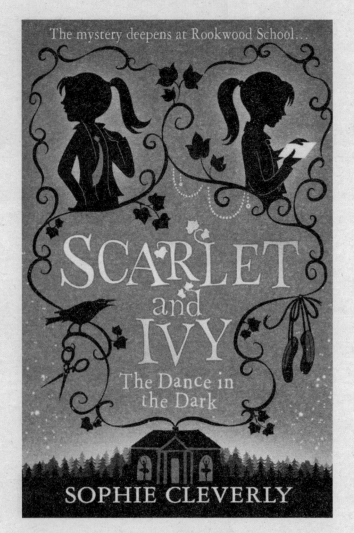